'80

Sadie Shapiro's
KNITTING BOOK

A NOVEL BY

ROBERT KIMMEL SMITH

SIMON AND SCHUSTER · NEW YORK

For
Sally and Edith
and
Sadie and Esther

Sadie Shapiro's
KNITTING BOOK

Somewhere on her desk there had to be a pencil.

Marian Wall held two fingers in the margin of the black-bound manuscript to search through a litter of galley proofs, ashtrays, business cards, the remains of a liverwurst sandwich on rye toast, three book jacket layouts, five envelopes containing bill payments she had meant to mail last week, and assorted scraps of paper scribbled over with assorted notes and ideas, half of them forgotten now, the other half already incorporated into the various manuscripts she had edited in the past six weeks. A pencil. There had to be a pencil. She opened the center drawer of her desk. Underneath a jumble of emery boards, tissues, paper clips, plastic spoons and packets of sugar, a spot of yellow indicated a well-worn Mongol #2. Now for a scratch pad, bottom left-hand drawer. Now what was it she wanted to note?

Sighing, Marian put the pencil into the manuscript to hold her place and folded it closed. I have been working on too many gothic novels, she thought, not for the first time. After a while they all tend to merge and become one in your mind. The brave young heroines in danger, the old rotting mansions set in bleak landscapes, the mysterious (but handsome) young men who would either threaten or fall in love with the heroine, and sometimes would do both. Which was this one now? Oh, yes. *Midnight Mansion,* set in the Scottish Highlands, which made a nice change from the author's previous books set in Dorset, Cornwall, and the Irish Lowlands.

Turning in her swivel chair, Marian looked into the oval mirror that hung on the smudged cream wall. Thirty-three years old, she thought, and I hate my hair. She swept it back off her forehead and peered at the increasing strands of gray. Does she or doesn't she? She doesn't, and it shows. Next week, a haircut, a color rinse, a new dress . . . Stop kidding yourself, she decided, then blinked at her image in the mirror, tears just behind her lashes.

When the telephone rang, she was happy for the interruption.

"Is that you, Marian?" a soft male voice asked.

As Marian answered, she heard a quiet chuckle, and in that instant identified the caller. It was him again, the odd-ball admirer who had been calling her at home and in the office for more than two months. Heathcliff was the secret name Marian had given him after his first call.

"Oh, sweet Marian," the voice was saying.

"Please," Marian interrupted, "I don't have time right now."

"I will be there tonight, and when you open the door . . ."

I must call the supermarket, thought Marian, tuning the caller out. If you don't get your order in by three o'clock, they never have it ready when you stop by after work. She looked at her watch.

". . . and you'll be wearing something special . . . all white, by Galanos or Oscar de la Renta perhaps, with just a small diamond clip at your throat . . ."

Retrieving the pencil and losing her place in the manuscript, Marian began to make notes on the margin of the title page. Butter, eggs, Velveeta, a package of Ring Dings . . .

". . . and I'll sweep you up into my arms and hold you close for just an instant. Then I'll step back and look at you. I could do that for hours, you know that, don't you, Marian?"

Cantaloupe or honeydew? The last honeydew melon had

been overripe. She'd had to throw most of it away. Cantaloupe then. Or should she shop for fruit in the little stand across the street from the supermarket.

"You know that? Marian?"

"What?"

"How much I love to look at you. Did I tell you?"

"I think so, yes. When we were dancing on the George Washington Bridge. Last week."

There was a moment of silence from Heathcliff in which Marian decided to take a chance on the honeydew again. Laura, her eleven-year-old, preferred honeydew.

"I said that?"

"Said what?"

"About the bridge?"

"Yes. You had them stop the traffic for the evening, remember? And there were just the two of us, dancing on the George Washington Bridge—except for the New York Philharmonic, of course."

"I must be having a breakdown," Heathcliff said. "I don't recall saying any of that."

"Take my word for it," Marian said as the intercom buzzed softly. "Hold on, I've got another call." She punched the lighted button and Jack Gatewood was on the line. "Hey, Marian," he began, "it looks like this knitting thing is coming up to bat. Arnold buzzed me this morning—he likes the samples."

"Oh, no," Marian groaned.

"Oh, yes," Jack said, "Arnold's talking full speed ahead. So could you meet me in his office? In, say, five minutes?"

"Look, Jack, I don't want to edit that book. I told you and I told Arnold—"

"Tell him again, sweetie," Jack said. "We tee off in five minutes."

Oh, God, the knitting book. Now where had she put the correspondence file and the patterns?

3

"Where was I?" Heathcliff said, as Marian punched up his line.

"Standing back and admiring me."

"Right. And I'll be wearing tails, of course, and I'll whisk you out the door and we'll be off . . ."

Damn, the knitting book. They would gang up and stick her with the job for sure. Another "arts and crafts" book to edit, another thankless, demanding job that would go on and on until her brain turned to jelly. Because she was a woman, right? That's why she'd get stuck with the knitting book, just as she had been commandeered to do the crewel book and the book on paper-flower-making, not to mention her all-time hate: *Redecorating With Wallpaper*. Gothics and handicrafts, that was her lot at Harbor Press. A woman's place is in the office, editing books for women.

". . . in the back of a hansom cab, clip-clopping through Central Park as the twilight begins to fall, holding you in the curve of my arm and—"

"I've got to hang up now," Marian said.

"Come on," Heathcliff protested, "I'm just getting started."

"Really, I have to go."

"Well, I'll call you at home."

"Will you just look at these marvelous creations," Arnold Hawthorne was saying as he held aloft a brightly colored sweater knitted in an all-over paisley pattern. The portly publisher of Harbor Press ("Books for the Millions") winked at Jack Gatewood, his editor-in-chief. "I smell a big seller here, Jack, don't you agree?"

"It just could be," Gatewood said, shrugging casually and turning to smile at Marian who sat beside him on the nubby tweed couch.

"And to think it came from slush," Hawthorne went on. "Over the transom, from nobody." He shook his head in wonder. "I'll say this: whoever created these items is an absolute genius. I've never seen such sheer invention." He held up a small knitted oblong with three white buttons sewn on its upper surface. "Now this is fantastic, isn't it?" he said, looking closely at the item in his hand. "What the hell is it?"

I'm going to be stuck with it, Marian Wall thought sourly. We are going to publish this damned book, and I'm about to be elected fairy godmother. "It's a glove, Arnold," she said heavily, getting up and putting it on her small hand, "a child's mitten. These three buttons on top are the eyes and nose of an animal, see? And when the child opens its hand—like this—you see the animal's mouth, here on my palm, and the little pink tongue inside."

"Wonderful," Hawthorne said, "I've never seen anything like it. Are the other patterns this person submitted—Shapiro, isn't it?—are the other patterns as good?"

"Beats me," Jack Gatewood said, looking at Marian.

"Believe it or not," Marian said, "I can't tell either. I've never knitted a stitch in my life. All I know is that a package came to us marked Care of Publisher. You sent it to Jack, who sent it to Eustace, who shoved it on to Mace, who left it on my desk."

"We do tend to leave things on your desk," Jack Gatewood said.

"Precisely," said Marian. "Inside the package there were fifty knitting patterns and instructions, and these few samples. The sweater, the mittens, and these." She held up a pair of children's slippers knitted in heavy blue wool, with an elegant bow-tie worked in across the instep. "Plus the note, which you've already read."

"A rather inarticulate note, as I recall," said Hawthorne. "But then, if one spends one's time knitting . . ."

"Have you contacted this Mrs. Shapiro?" Jack asked.

"I haven't tried," Marian said. "Not until I was sure we were interested in the book."

"By all means do, then," said Hawthorne, waving a heavy hand. "The market for craft books is booming these days."

"Arnold," Marian said slowly, "I don't want to be the editor on this book."

"Marian, Marian," soothed the publisher.

"I mean it. I don't want to do it. All I ever seem to work on around here are gothics and handicrafts, and it's not enough. I'm a complete person, Arnold, besides being a woman, I mean."

"Come on, Marian," Gatewood said, "who else do we have?"

"I don't care who else you have," Marian said. "Give it to Eustace Fielding. Give it to Mace Masterman. Every good novel I find you give to them, anyway."

"She's off again," Jack said to Hawthorne.

"Darn right I'm off again. Who first read *Memoirs of a Painted Lady?* I did. And who got to work on it? Eustace Fielding."

"And how many copies did it sell?" said Hawthorne. "Nine hundred and forty."

"Marian, sweetie," Jack put in, "you've been carrying this operation on your back. You're our strength, our heavy hitter."

"I'm more like your dishrag," Marian said, folding her arms.

"Now, now, Marian," Hawthorne began. He regarded the bare spot worn into the carpet in front of his desk. "Those gothics of yours and Jack's sports books are what keep us going. And the craft books. Do you know how many copies of *Redecorating With Wallpaper* we've sold? Fifty-three thousand copies at nine ninety-five a copy. And two book clubs have taken it."

"Oh, God," said Marian wearily.

"If it weren't for you, we'd already be in porno," Jack said.

6

"Or worse," echoed Arnold Hawthorne, nodding. "Is there something worse than porno?"

Silent, Marian stared for a long moment into Jack Gatewood's gray-green eyes, looking for a sign. But that perfect sun-bronzed face was passive, as it almost always was. It was the face of a tennis pro, an Austrian ski instructor. No, more than that, it was the face of a movie star who would be cast in those parts.

"All right," she said with a good loser's smile. She knew in her heart that she had already agreed to do the knitting book, and any others that had to be done. Because she was weak, because she was a woman, because she was and always would be Marian Wall—the girl who had begun as a switchboard operator at Harbor Press and worked her way up. And because she knew she could never work her way up any higher.

"You win again," Marian said, turning to face Hawthorne. "The knitting book is mine."

"I knew you'd agree," said Hawthorne, beaming. "Find this Mrs. Shapiro and sign her." He made an expansive gesture with his hand. "Give her anything she wants for an advance—up to seven hundred and fifty dollars."

Marian collected the knitted samples, the interoffice correspondence and the handwritten note and walked slowly back to her office with Jack Gatewood. "You'll get in touch with this dame, then?" he said.

Marian nodded and put a smile on her face as Jack walked off. She looked idly at the samples in her hand, feeling depressed. Why do I always get to the point of threatening to leave and never say it? she asked herself. You know you can't afford it, she answered in the next instant. And what's more, you're afraid they'd let you quit, and then where would you be? Who would keep you and Laura afloat while you looked for another job? And how easy would it be to find one?

Crushed at reaching the real bedrock of her existence, Marian reread the note that had accompanied the knitting samples and patterns. "I don't know why I'm sending you this except I'm maybe one of the best knitters in America and maybe sometime you want to put out a book on knitting so we could get together. These are my best 50 patterns and if you don't like them just say so and I'll quick send you 50 more. Patterns I got (made up by me) and all of them original too. So let me know. If you don't like them we'll still be the same friends and you'll send me back and I'll pay the postage." The signature read: "Mrs. S. Shapiro," and below that was an address in Queens.

Marian dialed Information. There was no Shapiro listed at the address in the letter. In fact, there was only one phone number at the address. She dialed and waited through four rings. "Just wait a minute," a woman said when the phone was picked up, and then Marian heard her speaking to someone in a muffled voice.

"Hello," Marian said. "Mrs. S. Shapiro, please."

"You'll have to speak up, I don't hear too good," the woman said, "and besides, they're all playing bingo."

"Bingo?"

"We never disturb them in the Bingo Room except an emergency. A person needs maybe one number to make bingo, you know, and you go in—"

"Look—" Marian began.

"—and you can get your head handed to you if you call them away."

"Is there a Mrs. S. Shapiro there?"

"S.?" the woman said. "Oh, you must mean Sadie."

"Sadie?" said Marian. "Look, my name is Marian Wall and I'm with Harbor Press. Can you have Mrs. Shapiro call me back?"

"Ooops! There's the dinner chimes. I got to go now."

"Wait!" said Marian. "Who am I talking to? Is this a residence or a business firm?"

"You could say both. It's the Mount Eden Senior Citizens Hotel, and I don't want to be late for dinner."

2

~~~~~~~~~~~

"I wish I was in Ponce, olé, olé," Juan Otero sang softly to himself as his taxi crawled slowly along behind a Brunk-horst meat truck on the expressway. Stop and go, stop and go, brake lights winking in the blazing sun. Juan took a gray-yellow handkerchief from the seat and mopped his wet brow. June, hot, and a parkway that was solidly bumper-to-bumper. Mother of God, why had he ever left Puerto Rico? In Ponce the breezes would be blowing from the sea . . .

"Will it take much longer?" Marian Wall asked from the back seat.

"A year, maybe two," said Juan. He lowered his eyes to the rearview mirror and regarded the passenger he had picked up at the Grindl Building in Manhattan. Cold, he thought, very cold. She does not know of love or of passion. And that hair . . . "Is the Long Island Expressway," he said, shrugging in a characteristic gesture. He caught the woman's eyes in the mirror and flashed her a smile. "A curse of God because we dare to invent the automobile." His comment brought no more than a glassy stare from the eyes of the brown-haired lady. Ah, *muchacho,* there were some people who did not know a joke even when it tickled them under the chin. That chin, he thought, sneaking another long look. Not a bad chin, nor was her mouth especially forbidding. And the rest of the face, especially the upturned nose, could almost be called pretty.

"Maybe you ought to get off the expressway," Marian said.

10

"We don't seem to be moving and it's been an hour since we came through the tunnel."

"If you like, I get off," said Juan. He swung the taxi sharply into the right-hand lane, provoking an angry chorus of horns and a shaken fist from the driver of the panel truck that he had successfully cut off. "Do you know Queens?" he asked, swinging onto the exit ramp that led to Queens Boulevard.

"Not at all."

"Good. Then we get lost together."

"Forty-seven twenty-five Hollis Avenue," Marian said, and then repeated the number silently, as a kind of litany to hold back the more violent thoughts that raced along the fuzzy edge of her consciousness. The mountain is going to Mohammed, she was thinking, for a knitting book, no less. Why wouldn't the mysterious Mrs. Shapiro come into the city, have lunch, and discuss the project as any normal person would? And why, on the hottest June day the world had ever known, was she dragging herself to the Mount Eden Senior Citizens Hotel located in God-knows-where, Queens? Would Mace Masterman make such a trip? Damn right he wouldn't. Nor would Eustace Fielding, or Jack Gatewood, or any other editor in his right mind. Only you, Marian Wall. What a horrible way to make thirteen thousand dollars a year. Less withholding, Blue Cross, city and state taxes, F.I.C.A. (whatever that was) and the occasional United Fund contribution wrested from her at the point of a gun by Jack Gatewood.

(Never looking her in the eye, he would go on assertively: "It's a team effort, Marian, everyone getting behind the ball. We must have everyone contribute something, you see, because for a hundred per cent team effort there's this handsome plaque Arnold gets that goes on his wall.")

Publishing. Ech! How does a bright young girl, a Barnard

grad, magna cum laude, get into publishing? I just drifted into it because, well, what else does an English major do?

"Hey, lady," Juan said, smiling, "I think the numbers are running the wrong way."

Marian looked at the house numbers on the tree-lined street. They were at nine hundred and falling.

"I go back the other way," Juan said, swinging the yellow cab through an intersection and making the tires squeal.

"Are we near Hollis Avenue?"

"Who knows?" Juan shrugged. "Is a foreign country." He tuned the tiny portable radio on the dash to a Spanish-language station and settled back to "Un Poquito de Amor."

An English major. God, how those words had affected her life. That day, so long ago, in the coffee shop of the United Nations Building. The man, handsome but for his hawk nose, looking at her over his coffee cup as she transcribed notes for the thesis she was writing. "And what do you do?" he asked as she looked up, his eyes a muddy brown that matched the river flowing by just outside the window. Blushing like the schoolgirl she was, she stammered: "I am an English major."

"And I," he said, smiling, "am a French colonel."

Jean-Claude de Lattre Wall, of the *Département de la Loire* and the *Deuxième Bureau* was indeed, as it turned out, a colonel, and also a diplomat—but not too diplomatic to take her hand and hold it in his. Nor to read her fortune and future in his quiet voice, tracing the lines in her hand with a finger that tickled and yet did more. And the days that followed were as golden as his hair and filled with the tenderness of first love.

They were married in the small chapel at the United Nations, and when graduation time came, Marian was already pregnant under her flowing black gown. But even before Laura was born, the marriage had begun to come apart.

Jean-Claude's true love, Marian sorrowfully discovered, was alcohol in any form. Under its influence, which was almost constant, the gentle colonel was transformed into a monster who thought nothing of striking her in anger, nor of throwing things against the walls of their tiny apartment. Shortly after their final argument, punctuated by Jean-Claude's drunken shouts and Laura's tiny cries, the colonel disappeared into the Congo.

The colonel's diplomatic status made him immune, Marian soon learned, to American laws relating to the support of Laura. The secrets of the *Deuxième Bureau,* a high-ranking clerk assured her with a sage nod, extended even beyond the grave. And as for the Colonel Wall she was seeking, if indeed there actually existed a colonel with that name, or if it could be confirmed that he was in the service . . .

With only one more rent payment left in the bank, Marian began working as a switchboard operator at Harbor Press. A year later her divorce from Jean-Claude became final.

"I think we are getting there," Juan Otero called, bringing Marian back to the present. They were riding under an arch of green shade trees that bordered what appeared to be a park. On the side of the street opposite the park were small wood-frame homes, and from the numbers painted on the garbage cans that lined the sidewalk, Marian saw that forty-seven twenty-five lay not far ahead. "Are we on Hollis Avenue?" she asked.

"No," said Juan, "but I think it cannot be far away." He pulled to the curb at the next corner. "We ask someone now, okay?"

Through a window Marian could see coming toward them a strange figure. A woman? Yes, a woman, in a shaggy suit of bright pink. A *sweat suit?* The woman was no more than fifty yards away. Yes, it was a sweat suit, Marian could see now, and the woman was jogging, or at least bouncing slowly up and down as she made slight forward progress. A tiny wisp of an old woman, with gray-white hair peeping out from under her matching pink tam, and on her nose a pair of silver-rimmed sunglasses.

"What is she doing?" Juan asked. "Is she *loco?*"

"Jogging, I think," said Marian. "I'll ask her for directions," she said as she stepped from the cab. "Excuse me . . ."

The old woman drew abreast of the taxi and held up a small hand. "Wait," she managed to say between gasps, leaning against the cab, her head held down. The pink sweat suit was knit, Marian observed, and beautifully designed in an overall diamond pattern. On the back of the loose-fitting jacket an emblem had been worked into the design. It looked something like a wheel, Marian thought; then on closer examination she saw that it was, in fact, a kind of wheelchair. Under the spokes of the wheels were the letters M.E.S.C.H.

"Hollis Avenue," Marian said, "forty-seven twenty-five Hollis Avenue. Is it near here?"

The old woman was still gasping for air, but she managed to nod. "Hold on a second," she said, her small chest heaving. Drawing a dainty lace handkerchief from the sweat suit's breast pocket, she mopped her brow. "A mile and a half I jogged," she wheezed, then consulted her wristwatch. "In only an hour and ten minutes." At this the woman smiled broadly, then suddenly took a half step backward, staggered as if she would fall and draped herself across the taxi's front fender in a half-swoon, the breath pouring from her as from a punctured balloon. Her small pink face turned chalk-white and her eyelids began to flutter.

Marian bounded to her side, grasping the woman's bony hand, as Juan hastily scrambled out of the cab to help. "Are you all right?" Marian asked anxiously. She fanned the air above the old woman's face with her patent-leather handbag.

"Don't be afraid," the old woman said haltingly. "It's only

14

my heart and maybe my liver." She ran her free hand across her mid-section. "Of course, my gall bladder isn't what it used to be . . . and my hiatus hernia . . . but that's an old story already." She began to lift her head, then thought better of it and reclined across the fender. "Then again," she went on, "it could have been lunch. You know, you eat fatty pot roast . . . Believe me, what they don't know about trimming a piece of meat. You ever have somebody serve you a pot roast sandwich all fat? My worst enemies should have to eat what they give you."

"Take it easy," Marian said. "Just relax."

"And then you go and jog a mile and a half on top of a meal like that, you got to have your head examined, right? Not to mention your heart and the rest of what's inside."

"And in this heat," Marian nodded.

"Heat, shmeat," the woman said. She lifted her head, looking somewhat stronger, and managed to sit half-erect upon the fender. "You let a little heat stop you, or a little cold or rain, you know what happens? You end up sitting in a chair by the window, that's what. From this I know plenty. Listen, who else is going to take care of your body if you don't? Rockefeller? Just sitting around and playing bingo or maybe mah-jongg, you don't stay healthy. Believe me, a lot of people my age are dead already.

"Help me up," she said, extending a hand to Marian. With Marian gently tugging, the old woman managed to get to her feet. "Every other day I jog. Rain or shine or snow or cold or whatever. Listen, I heard about a man in one of those big cities in Australia . . . what do you call it?"

"Sydney?"

"I don't know his name. Anyway, the man is ninety-two years of age, and he jogs a hundred miles a week. *A hundred miles a week*, can you believe that?"

"No."

"Neither can I, but I'll bet you he's in some terrific shape."

At this the old woman thrust her hands skyward and took a deep breath, then plunged toward the ground. Alarmed, Marian reached out to her, and then stopped as the woman performed a perfectly respectable deep knee bend and came back to her feet, smiling. "All right," she said, "good as new. Thank God I won't have to jog again until the day after tomorrow."

"Are you all right now?" Marian asked, a little hesitantly.

"Fine, fine. As good as a person seventy-two or seventy-five years old has a right to feel." She clutched Marian's arm and squeezed it gently. "Don't worry, and thanks for being so sweet and worrying about me. Not everyone shows feelings, you know. You could drop down dead on the street today, and people would just step right over you, and that's your America." Adjusting her tam and setting her sunglasses straight, the woman prepared to march off.

"Wait, lady," said Juan. "I'm looking for the Mount Eden Senior Citizens Hotel."

"Around the corner." A sudden smile brightened her face as she looked closely at Marian. "There's a woman coming to see me today. From Manhattan . . . a book publisher . . ."

Oh, sweet Lord, Marian thought, please don't let it be. "Are you . . . Sadie Shapiro?"

"The same," said Sadie Shapiro, "and you must be Marian Wall." Taking off her sunglasses, Sadie favored Marian with a broad smile, the corners of her bright blue eyes crinkling. "Pay off the cabman, cookie," she said, "we can walk it from here. Unless . . . you wouldn't want to jog a little, would you?"

~~~~~~~~~~~~~~~~~~~~~~~

The Mount Eden Senior Citizens Hotel is a three-story, modern-looking structure set in a grove of stately elms on a quiet street. From the street the building looks immaculately whitewashed and clean. It is only when one gets close that the cracks in its facade are visible. A concrete loggia projects over the building's circular driveway, and in its shade a group of elderly men and women sat talking among themselves as Sadie and Marian approached. Marian was acutely aware of their eyes and of the unabashed manner in which they looked her up and down, noting her hair style, her stride, the length and cut of her jersey dress, her shoes, her handbag, and the absence of a wedding band on the ring finger of her left hand.

"So, Sadie," one of the women called as they drew near, "how far did you run today?"

"A mile and a half."

"Is that a normal person?" a man in a wheelchair remarked, shaking his head.

"Who said she's normal?" his companion replied. "A person thinks she's Wonder Woman is not a normal person."

"Listen," said a woman with blue hair, "you know when she'll be happy? When she kills herself, then she'll be happy." This remark precipitated a general clacking of tongues and shaking of heads among the group.

"Keep moving," Sadie confided *sotto voce* as she led Marian toward the doorway. "One word and we'll be here all day."

The lobby was frigidly air-conditioned and circular in shape. A clutter of overstuffed chairs and French-Provincial divans, all of them slipcovered in yellowing plastic, were arranged in conversational groupings. The walls were done in shiny gold-striped wallpaper, interrupted here and there with imitation Miro tapestries in primary colors. The floor was terrazzo, or its vinyl equivalent, inset with shiny brass fleurs-de-lis. The central focus of the lobby, however, was an immense crystal chandelier hanging stage-center, its ropes of crystal beads set off by what seemed scores of Disney-like brass cherubs, each little cherub carrying a flame-shaped electric light bulb on his back.

"How do you like it?" Sadie asked, a small smile playing about her lips.

"Interesting," said Marian, hoping not to offend.

"The Fontainebleau *North,* we call it."

Across the lobby a pair of elevator doors creaked open, and a tall, spare man, wearing white slacks and a blazing red golf shirt emerged. Spotting Sadie, he waved and came walking up, a king-sized cigar clenched in his teeth. "So," he said, ignoring Marian for the moment, "how far did we jog today?"

"A mile and a half."

"In how long?"

"An hour and ten minutes."

The man's thick white eyebrows rose in what might have been surprise, and he took the cigar from his mouth just long enough to flick an inch of ash to the floor. "Terrific," he said. "I'm going to send a challenge to Kip Keino. Next year, the Olympics."

A wide smile was on Sadie's lips as she turned to Marian. "Marian Wall, I'd like you to meet Mr. Sam Beck, a special friend of mine."

"Who would like to be even more special and a lot more

18

friendly," Beck said, grasping Marian's hand. "And you must be the publishing lady."

"How do you do," Marian said.

"I used to be in publishing myself, a long time ago."

"Really?" Marian said, smiling.

"Had a newsstand on Broadway and Seventy-second Street."

"That was when Hector was a pup," said Sadie.

"And Manhattan was a prairie," nodded Beck. "So tell me, have you made Sadie an offer yet?"

"Not yet."

"Good luck," said Beck. "I make Sadie an offer about once a week."

"Sam!" Sadie whispered.

"Hasn't taken me up on it yet," he said dryly.

"Well," said Marian, somewhat at a loss, "we do intend to publish Mrs. Shapiro's book. I'm here to work out the details."

"Ah-hah," said Beck. He nudged Sadie's elbow. "I've been trying to work out the details with Sadie for two years now."

"Sam," said Sadie, a pink flush on her cheeks.

"Such a small detail, too," Beck said. He blew a smoke ring at the chandelier, then looked at Marian. "You always wear your hair that way?"

"Yes. Is there something wrong?"

"No," Beck shrugged, "just asking." Behind the cigar he flashed Marian a crooked smile.

"Sam," cautioned Sadie, "behave yourself."

"I'm seventy-seven years old," Beck said. "There's no percentage in behaving myself." He winked at Sadie. "Light of my life, I hear there's going to be a full moon tonight. You want to come up to my room and listen to Artie Shaw records?"

"We were just leaving," said Sadie, taking Marian's arm.

"I'll show you my violin, Sadie."

"And then we'll fiddle around," Sadie and Sam Beck said simultaneously.

"Bye, Sam," Sadie said with a flirtatious wave as she led Marian away. "The sweetest man in the whole place," she observed when they were out of earshot. "So full of life, and he keeps himself so nice. You wouldn't think he had a prostate about five years ago, would you?"

They walked across the lobby and passed by an easel holding a scroll that proclaimed in Old English lettering "Grandchildren of the Month." Four candid color-snaps of smiling children were affixed to the face of the easel, and beneath each photo a typewritten card noted name, age, and grandfilial affiliation. "The Grandmothers' Club," said Sadie frostily. "Can you imagine an organization of women that all they do is sit around and tell stories about their grandchildren? And if you're not a member, they don't put up your pictures."

"And you're not a member?"

"I'm not an anything," said Sadie. "Come on, I'll show you around." She opened a door off the lobby and led Marian into a large dining room that looked into a sunny back garden. "Where the elite meet to eat," said Sadie.

"Very nice."

"You haven't eaten here." In an adjoining room a group of perhaps a dozen women sat at card tables. They looked up as Sadie and Marian passed through the room, and a few of them nodded. "The Bridge Club," Sadie whispered. "They only take time out to eat and sleep." A connecting door led into a dark carpeted corridor off which there proved to be a social room, a small music chamber, and a minuscule library stocked mostly with paperbacks. Yet another door led them back to the lobby. "You've spoken to Bertha," Sadie said, pausing in front of the reception desk. "Bertha!" she shouted in a voice so loud it startled Marian. "Bertha!"

A face that might have been Grandma Moses' peeked out

from behind the switchboard, a telephone headset crowning the gray hair. "Hello, Sadie," Bertha said, smiling.

"This is my friend, Marian Wall," Sadie shouted.

The woman nodded. "On the ball," she said.

"Bertha Maloney, our telephone lady," said Sadie.

"How do you do," nodded Marian.

"Anytime," said Bertha Maloney.

"Poor woman," said Sadie as they walked toward the elevators. "She makes up a little on the rent here by working the switchboard."

"I see. Are there other tenants here who—"

"Guests," Sadie corrected. "Adolph Hitler insists we call ourselves guests, not tenants."

"Hitler?"

"Max Adolphus, the so-called manager. He's not what you'd call one of my friends. Although, come to think of it, there aren't more than a handful of people here I'd call friends anyway."

The elevator doors creaked open, and an aged man with yellow skin held the door as Marian and Sadie entered. The man was wearing a uniform that was remarkable for its antiquity and the fact that emblazoned above its breast pocket were the words "Roxy Theater." With a shaking hand he closed the elevator gate behind them and started the car upward with a jerk. "Again she's wearing the pink sweat suit," he muttered under his breath. "If it's not pink, it's red. Wouldn't wear a green sweat suit, or, God forbid, a red-white-and-blue one. Rotten Commonist."

"You see, Marian," Sadie said, ignoring the old man, "everything at Mount Eden is a click. You saw the Bridge Club downstairs. Then there's your mah-jongg group, and your bingo group, not to mention canasta and kalooki. The same women all the time, playing the same games, and saying the same things."

"And you don't play cards?"

"What I do mainly is stick to my knitting. Oh, that doesn't mean that I'm an outcast or I don't try to be friendly. Listen, when I first got here I plunged right in, trying to make friends, you know, and be one of the girls. But I found out that, for me at least, it was a mistake."

The elevator jerked to a stop, and Sadie showed Marian down a narrow hallway. She paused at her door and drew close to Marian. "I think my roommate, Mrs. Frankel, may be in. She's a little . . . what should I say? Not *all there*, if you take my meaning. So just nod and smile and don't pay too much attention, all right?"

"Of course."

"She means well," Sadie added, opening the door.

To Marian, the room appeared to be straight out of a Holiday Inn. Except for the hospital-type beds and the oxygen and paging plugs on the wall. On the bed nearest the casement windows, Mrs. Frankel lay sleeping. Her mouth was open and she was snoring quietly. "Make yourself comfortable," Sadie said in a low voice, indicating an upholstered chair. She took a housecoat from a sliding-door closet and disappeared into the bathroom. To the accompaniment of Mrs. Frankel's snores and the sound of Sadie's shower, Marian explored the cramped double room, trying to picture what it might be like to live in such a place. It was impossible to imagine, of course, a *grotesquerie,* and Marian wondered why Mrs. Shapiro had chosen such a life. Or had it been chosen for her? On top of a dresser was a color photograph. Two teen-agers on a beach, with palm trees. Florida, perhaps? Behind the children in the photograph was Sadie, seated on a deck chair, and next to her a man and a woman, the children's parents by the smiles they displayed. Sadie's son? It was possible. His eyes narrowed at the corners as Sadie's did, and there was an overall shrewdness about his face—in his strong mouth and sharply defined nose—that bespoke a Shapiro inheritance.

"Fatahyu duhn here?" a voice said, and Marian whirled to face an awakened Mrs. Frankel. The woman was sitting upright on her bed, a wild look on her face. *"Fatyu vant?"*

Alarmed, Marian took a backward step toward the door. "I'm a friend of Mrs. Shapiro. Sadie's friend."

The bathroom door opened a foot or so, and Sadie's head, wrapped in a green towel, appeared. She spoke sharply to Mrs. Frankel. "Calm yourself, Bessie. She's with me, a friend. Go back to sleep." She looked at Marian. "Just answer her, whatever she says. I'll be with you in two minutes." With that, she closed the door.

Mrs. Frankel sat staring at Marian, her face alert and somehow frightened-looking, her toothless mouth working silently. Uncomfortable, Marian sought a meeting ground. She commented on the weather, complimented the appearance of the room, and asked after Mrs. Frankel's health before the woman spoke again. "Shudall bah bed," she said heatedly, then repeated the phrase.

"Yes," Marian said, sensing that Mrs. Frankel sought agreement.

"Bah bed de hull bunch."

Marian nodded, wishing Sadie would hurry. There was something wild about the look in Mrs. Frankel's eyes, something naked and without defenses.

Sadie stepped confidently from the bathroom, a brightly printed floral housecoat wrapped about her small figure. "Why are you standing?" she said to Marian. "Sit down, relax."

"Fatah she duhn here?" Mrs. Frankel demanded.

"Bessie, dear," said Sadie with a patient sigh, "please put your teeth in." Mrs. Frankel's hand flew to her gaping mouth and covered it. "I told her a million times, you talk without your teeth, it comes out Hungarian."

Mrs. Frankel turned her face away from Marian and

swung off the bed. Walking sidewise, she disappeared into the bathroom.

"Was she cursing her family to you?" Sadie asked.

"I don't know," Marian shrugged. "I couldn't understand her."

"That Bessie, everybody she meets she starts cursing her daughters for putting her in this place." Shucking her knitted mules, a more sophisticated version of the children's slippers Marian had seen as samples, Sadie stretched out slowly on the bed. "A half-hour on my back and I'll be myself again. Marian, sit down, here by the bed. Relax, cookie, don't stand there like a stick. That's better," she went on when Marian had seated herself. "Now we should talk over about the knitting book, right? So fire ahead, I'm nothing but ears."

Marian opened her attaché case and looked for the file folder she had brought. Before she found it, however, Bessie Frankel emerged from the bathroom. She smiled at Sadie and pointed to her mouth.

"Terrific," said Sadie, "every tooth a gem."

"They should all drop dead, right?" Bessie said.

"Should stink from their heads," Sadie said amiably.

"Three daughters, you give them a lifetime, they end up packing their mother off like a steamer trunk." Bessie looked to Marian for agreement. "Is this right, I ask you?"

Marian stared for a moment, then caught Sadie's emphatic nod. "It's not right," she said.

"What did I tell you?" Bessie said, her chin thrust forward dramatically.

"They don't deserve your little pinkie," Sadie said.

"They should be like a chandelier," trumpeted Bessie. "Should hang in the daytime and burn at night."

"You're a hundred percent right."

"Of course I'm right," said Bessie. "Such a heartache from children I wouldn't wish on anyone." She smiled in a satisfied way, then sighed heavily.

"Bessie, darling," Sadie began, "I'd like to talk over something important with my friend, Mrs. Wall. So maybe you'll be an angel and go downstairs to the garden for a while?"

Bessie's mouth worked silently and her eyebrows rose. "So who would stay where she's not wanted?" she sniffed. Turning on her heel, she left the room.

Marian looked long and questioningly at Sadie. "Does she really hate her children so?"

"Hate them?" Sadie smiled. "She *loves* them. If they asked, she'd move in with any one of them in a minute."

"But the way she went on . . . those curses . . ."

"Only a habit. She doesn't mean a thing by it. In fact, she forgot one today. About they should live to lose all their teeth but one, and in that one tooth they should have a terrible toothache. It's like a regular routine. But you should see when her children come to visit on Sunday. Bessie is the happiest person in the world. Of course, as soon as they leave, she starts cursing them again."

"I don't understand."

"Listen, darling," Sadie said patiently, "we all have our ways and that's it. You can make a federal case out of it, or you can live with it. I lived with my son Stuart and his wife for three years after my Reuben died, he should find eternal peace. And what happened? My daughter-in-law and I drove each other crazy. I'm a neat person, I think you can tell that, but she . . . Well, I wouldn't exactly call her a slob, but the best housekeeper in the world she isn't. Not that I want to talk badly about her, mind you. But by me you don't wash a floor with a mop. That's not what I call clean. After all, if God didn't want us to scrub floors, why would he make scrub brushes?

"And you don't serve a child a Yankee Doodle they should put it on a napkin and get crumbs all over the table. I mean, even the Chinese know about cake plates, right? So what was going to be the answer? To fight like cats and dogs forever, or to move out and let her live the way she likes, and me to be myself also?"

Not realizing that Sadie's question was rhetorical, Marian began to answer, only to be cut off as Sadie drew breath and continued.

"So I moved up here to Mount Eden, and believe me, my daughter-in-law and I have been the best of friends ever since. And since she and my Stuart moved to Coral Gables, we've been even closer.

"And meanwhile, I'm happy here. I mean, Mount Eden isn't exactly the Ritz, but for what it is, it's all right. After all, a person like me, seventy-two or seventy-five years old, she doesn't have to do her own cooking any more, or cleaning, or shopping. And if she wants to be with people a little, or be by herself, and maybe go out to see a movie or even spend the whole day on her knitting, who is there to say no?"

The word "knitting" struck a chord, and Marian suddenly realized that from the moment she had met Sadie Shapiro she had spent not one second talking about the business that had brought her to Mount Eden. "Mrs. Shapiro," Marian said, "the knitting book. The samples you sent."

"You liked them, I know you did. After all, what was there not to like? Of course, if you want more I can go right into my big loose-leaf in the closet and show you three, four hundred others."

"No," said Marian. "I mean yes. I mean . . . wait a minute."

"Listen, darling, take your time. I already know you must like what I sent you because, after all, you didn't *shlep* all the way out here to Mount Eden for your health, right?"

Marian gazed at Sadie's recumbent figure and felt a sudden weariness. The myriad details of preparing a complicated book for publication, the months and months of work, and the dozens of meetings she would have to live through with Sadie Shapiro towered before her. "Mrs. Shapiro," she began, "we do want to produce your book. All of us at Harbor Press are convinced of your knitting skill, and we believe you're just the person who could—"

"What did I tell you?" said Sadie. "Absolutely right."

". . . but that's only the beginning. There are many details we'll have to attend to . . ."

"Listen, you know who you're talking to? Maybe the best knitter in America, that's all."

"I'm sure," said Marian. She opened the file folder in her lap and took out the work sheet she had prepared.

"A Sadie come-lately I'm not. It's maybe fifty years I've been knitting. I started, I remember, when I was carrying Stuart . . . and I wanted to make him something . . . you know, booties, maybe a little sweater, something. I mean, it wasn't like today where you walk into a store you got the whole world laid out in front of you. So I started knitting then, you see, for the baby that was coming, and with my Reuben working nights, what else was there to do without a TV or even a radio? I started out buying every pattern I could find—there wasn't a lot—but I made them all. What didn't I make? Hats, mufflers, gloves, sweaters. I made matching coats for the baby, Reuben, and myself in a powder blue wool I remember the color of it to this day. I made tea cozies even though I never used them, afghans, blankets, lap robes. I'm telling you, I became some crazy knitter. Pretty soon I'd knitted everything there was to knit until I couldn't find a pattern I hadn't made already. So I began to make up my own. Carriage covers, fancy tablecloths, slipcovers for the furniture. And then I went back to hats, gloves, mufflers and sweaters—new ones, my own designs. I made neckties for Reuben, and knitted shirts until he complained they itched him in the hot weather. Knitting was my magnificent obsession—if you remember that picture, which I'm sure you don't because you're only a young girl."

"Mrs. Shapiro . . ."

27

"Listen, if I had been smart enough to open a knitting store, I would be a rich woman today."

". . . we have a lot to discuss."

"The money I spent on wool alone, your best friends, Marian, should have such money."

"Please, Mrs. Shapiro," said Marian more loudly than she had intended. A look of surprise crossed Sadie's face, but she stopped speaking. "I'm sorry," Marian continued, "but you must let me go on for a few minutes without interrupting."

Sadie sighed heavily and lay back on the bed. "All right."

"Good. Now, first of all . . ."

"From this minute I'm as quiet as a carp."

"Fine. Let's talk about your contract. There'll be a small advance payment for you when you sign the contract. The balance of the advance money will be paid upon delivery of an acceptable manuscript."

"Not another word, so help me."

"Right," said Marian, sailing on before Sadie gathered a head of steam. Speaking at twice her normal rate, Marian explained the serpentine series of steps involved in creating the book and bringing it to market. Through it all Sadie lay quietly on the bed, her eyes bright, her lips grimly sealed. "We had in mind an advance payment of seven hundred and fifty dollars. Two hundred and fifty dollars on signing the contract, the balance as I stated before. Is that satisfactory?"

Sadie's compressed lips seemed to smile, but she said nothing.

"Mrs. Shapiro? . . . Sadie?"

"Now I can talk?" Sadie asked, an angelic look on her face.

A heavy stone shifted position inside Marian's chest. "Yes," she said, her voice under control. "Is it satisfactory?"

"Two hundred fifty dollars," Sadie said. "Seven hundred fifty dollars?" She sat up and swung her legs off the bed. "Believe me, Marian, forty-four cents would be enough. Nothing, even!" She pointed a manicured index finger and wagged her gray head. "You must think I'm doing this for money. You know what I say to money? I say 'phooey' to money!"

"I see, but—" was all Marian was able to reply before Sadie was on her feet.

"Why did I send you my patterns?" Sadie began rhetorically as she paced across the room. "Why did I collect knitting ideas ever since I was a young girl? It's a long, long story . . ."

And it was.

4

~~~~~~~~~~~~~~~~~~~~~~~~~~~~~

Here comes ninety-seven pounds of trouble, Max Adolphus was thinking as he spied Sadie Shapiro striding toward him across the lobby. Turning away swiftly before she could catch his eye, the obese manager of the Mount Eden Senior Citizens Hotel retreated to his office and closed the door behind him. Two seconds later, there was a knock, followed by a Sadie Shapiro. "Could I talk?"

"Whatever it is, the answer is no," Adolphus said. "Look, Shapiro, it's not even nine o'clock in the morning. I haven't had my breakfast yet."

"With you that's a blessing," Sadie retorted, grinning at the paunch overhanging the manager's alligator belt.

"All right," Adolphus said irritably, waving a pudgy hand. Why did I ever allow this woman to live here, he thought. Before she came, Mount Eden was a paradise, a hotel that ran smoothly, with a minimum of complaints from the residents and a maximum of profit for the owners, including himself. But now it was more difficult to cut corners, to economize on food and laundry and staff. The woman was an eagle eye, a rebel who stirred up trouble. And now she had attracted a group of followers and made complainers out of them, too. Their number was small, true, but it was growing.

"Talking a jogging team—" Sadie began.

"What? Again?" said Adolphus, cutting her off. "I told you last week, no jogging team. I won't have it."

"Last week you brushed me under the carpet, Adolphus. You gave me some nifty-swifty doubletalk, and I was out of here in two minutes. Now I *really* want to know why you won't even let me get started on this idea."

Adolphus stared at the wiry bundle of energy standing in front of his desk and tried hard to control his anger. He must not let her get through to him, he knew, and yet it was difficult. He picked up a round brass paperweight and rolled it in his hand. "All right, let me repeat what I said. Number one, you're talking about old people, Shapiro. Sick, too, a lot of them . . ."

"All the more reason for exercise."

". . . twenty-seven diabetics, forty-three hardening of the arteries. If we count arthritis and rheumatism, you can add a lot more. Now let's get serious. We got about sixty men and women who've had a minimum of one heart attack apiece. You start a messing around with jogging, and so help me they'll be dropping like flies."

"Wrong. I told you last week—jogging means you train the body—not strain it. I'm talking exercise, Adolphus, mild exercise which is terrific for the heart and lungs. You got in your mind a track meet, which is wrong."

Adolphus sighed and squeezed the paperweight.

"We got already a croquet team and a ping-pong tournament. So why not jogging?"

"Croquet and ping-pong don't require exertion," said Adolphus. "Jogging is heavy exercise."

"Not if you do it right," Sadie insisted. "I could show you a whole bunch of articles, including the *Reader's Digest*—"

"Look, Shapiro, no jogging. Please don't waste my time with this nonsense."

"Putting extra years on people is not nonsense. If you would know how wonderful jogging makes you feel, even you would try it, which from the looks of it is not a bad idea."

"I'll ignore that," said Adolphus. "Look, we have a regularly scheduled exercise class . . ."

"Which only three people turn out for, and you know it. 'Muscles' Manfredi, who used to be a weightlifter and likes to show off his body, Mildred Futterman, who weighs three hundred pounds, and Mr. Schwartz, who's only going because he wants to get next to Mildred Futterman."

"That's not true, Shapiro. We have a bigger turnout than that."

"Mostly men," said Sadie, "and all they're doing is watching Mildred Futterman bend over. That's not exercise, except for eyeballs. Now with jogging, we'd get a whole different crowd of people."

"You don't give up, do you?" said Adolphus, sitting back in his chair.

"I'll knit them sweat suits like mine, in coordinated colors. You saw the emblem on the back of my jogging suit, right? Could you want nicer than that?"

"No jogging team. Absolutely not."

"Besides, I already talked to the people at Fidelman's Retirement Haven, and they got a jogging team, Adolphus. And they said maybe we can even get together, go on outings and have some fun. So how about it?"

Adolphus stiffened, as he always did when the name of Fidelman, Mount Eden's nearby competitor, was mentioned. "All right, Shapiro, I'll level with you. I've consulted with our medical authority, and he has said *no*. So that's your answer."

"Medical authority?" Sadie repeated. "You mean Schultz? 'Cockeye' Schultz, that quack?"

"Now just a minute," said Adolphus with some heat. "Dr. Schultz is an eminent man . . . a recognized authority in the field of geri—"

"He wouldn't know a case of lockjaw if it bit him on the finger," Sadie interrupted. "And besides, he's a part owner here. Some medical authority."

A pink glow began to spread upward from Adolphus' chins to his round cheeks.

"What if I put up a note on the bulletin board? Would it hurt to ask if people are interested?"

"You put up a sign and I'll take it down," Adolphus barked. "Unauthorized use of the bulletin board is against the rules."

"Hoo-ha, am I scared."

Before Adolphus could reply, a series of chimes sounded. "Last call to breakfast," the manager said with relief. He pushed out from behind the desk and brushed past Sadie. "If you'll excuse me . . ."

"Go ahead. Have a few Danish with butter, they'll do you good," Sadie said, smiling.

In the doorway, Adolphus turned. "I'm warning you, Shapiro. You signed an agreement when you came here. Violate the rules and you're out. Just remember that."

"And I'm warning you, Adolphus," Sadie said. "There's no rule against a person being herself. What you'd like around here is zombies. Quiet little people you can step all over and do what you like. But I was born with a mind and a mouth, and I'm going to use them until the day I die."

A malevolent grin creased Adolphus' face. "That can't be too soon," he growled, then turned and waddled off toward the dining room.

Sadie watched Max Adolphus' retreating figure. Someday, she repeated to herself without taking the thought further, someday . . . Regaining control, she walked to the desk. "Bertha!" she called out three times. The telephone operator's smiling visage peeked out from behind the switchboard after yet another summons. "Did you get the mail?" Sadie asked.

"Who's in jail?" Bertha asked in turn.

"The mail," Sadie said patiently, "you know, letters?" She mimed opening an envelope and reading a letter.

"Oh, yah," said Bertha, brightening, "you got a big one this morning." She looked through a stack of letters and handed a bulky envelope across the counter.

Sadie looked at the return address. "Hey! It's from Harbor Press. I'll bet it's my contract." She opened the envelope and withdrew a bulky five-page document bound in blue paper. "It is. Oh, boy! I got to show this to Sam Beck." Whirling with delight, Sadie trotted across the lobby and into the dining room, passing the manager's table without so much as a glance. At his usual table near the garden windows, Sam Beck sat sipping coffee and smoking a cigar. Seated with him were Bessie Frankel and Abe Farkas, Beck's partner at cards.

"Here it is," Sadie announced, drawing up a chair. "My contract. From Harbor Press." She waved the document in the air like a wand.

"Calm down before you drop it in my coffee," Beck said. He reached out and took the contract from Sadie. Withdrawing a pair of eyeglasses from the breast pocket of his burgundy blazer, he placed them on the end of his nose and began to read. "How do you like that?" he grinned at Sadie. "It's a real contract. They weren't kidding. Sadie, love, they really want to publish your book."

"Yes."

Sam lifted his coffee cup in a toast. "Congratulations, my author," he said. "Sadie, this is wonderful."

"I know," said Sadie. "I'm so excited inside, I'm jumping up and down."

"Lots of luck," Abe Farkas said.

"*Mazeltov*," said Bessie Frankel from behind a spoonful of farina.

"Thank you," said Sadie, smiling for all she was worth. She leaned over and pecked Sam on the cheek.

"How do you do?" he said, raising his eyebrows. "Now I know you're excited."

"Don't get carried away," Abe Farkas said. "No kissing at breakfast."

"Never mind that," said Sadie. "Who's got a pen? I want to sign this right away and send it back this afternoon. Before they change their minds."

"Not so fast, Sadie," Abe Farkas said, wagging his head. "Forty-seven years in dry goods, I learned one thing. Look before you leap, and don't sign anything without reading it."

"He's right," Sam said. "You ought to at least look this over before you sign it. After all, it's a contract. Who knows what they put in there? It could be tricky."

"Who tricky? What tricky? This is Harbor Press. They're a big outfit, aren't they?"

"Never heard of them," said Farkas.

"Neither did I," Sadie confessed, "except for one book, *Redecorating With Wallpaper*. Which is why I sent them my samples in the first place."

"I'd have a good lawyer look it over before I signed it," Sam said.

"So who's got a lawyer?" Sadie asked.

"I've got one, but I wouldn't recommend him," Sam Beck said. He took a sip of coffee and glanced into the garden.

"My youngest daughter is married to a lawyer," Bessie Frankel said. "He should lift a Volkswagen and get a hernia."

"Is he a good lawyer?" Beck asked.

"He's not a good anything," said Bessie.

"Maybe I should just sign it," said Sadie.

"No, no," said Beck. "It should be looked at by a professional." His eyebrows furrowed with concentration as he drew on his cigar. "Wait a minute. We've got a lawyer right on the premises. Rosenbloom."

"Who's Rosenbloom?" asked Farkas.

"The little guy, sits over in the far corner of the dining room. He walks with a cane, got a tic in his cheek, and he's on a salt-free diet. I was talking to him the other day, while

35

we were handicapping the horses. If I remember right, he said he used to be on Wall Street."

"That's the best kind of lawyer," said Farkas.

"He's your man, Sadie," Beck said. He put the contract in the inside pocket of his blazer. "Leave it to me. You're in good hands with Sam Beck . . . although these hands could use some more of you to be good to."

Before Sadie could reply, there was the sound of shouting from the middle of the room. Sadie turned just in time to see Max Adolphus giving a tongue-lashing to Carlos, the much overworked busboy. Catching Sadie's eyes upon him, Adolphus glared.

"What's he mad at you for?" Sam asked.

"I don't know," Sadie said, "and I don't care. I'm going to have a book soon, Sam. A book, with my name on it. Nothing can bother me now."

5

Two sticky weeks later, the matter of Sadie's contract was still unresolved.

Rosenbloom, the little guy from the far corner of the dining room, had proved to be Harold R. Rosenbloom, former head of the contract department of Weymouth and Lazard, a giant industrial holding company. There were "one or two minor points" that might be negotiated, he had told Sam Beck after reading the contract over. Sadie, of course, had very much wanted to sign it at once and send it back to Marian, but Sam insisted that Rosenbloom be given an opportunity to work in her behalf. And because Sadie had come to value Sam Beck's opinion, she listened to him.

Thus it was that Marian found herself once more in the backwoods of Queens on the way to Mount Eden, a journey she had promised herself she would never make again. The parties involved were waiting for her in Mount Eden's library, and Sadie made the introductions.

"I'm very happy to meet you," said Harold Rosenbloom with a courtly half-bow. The diminutive lawyer was wearing a conservative charcoal-gray three-button suit with a vest, in marked contrast to Sam Beck's canary yellow sports shirt and slacks. "I'm sorry if we've inconvenienced you by making you take another trip out here. Our points of disagreement are small, as you know."

"That's all right," said Marian, calling upon reserves of patience she did not know she possessed.

37

"In two minutes we'll be finished with this, and then we'll all have some iced tea," said Sadie brightly.

"Let us hope so," Rosenbloom said with a small smile. He took up the blue-bound contract and began to read it aloud.

I can't believe he's going to read the whole thing, thought Marian. She looked at Rosenbloom, whose horn-rims perched upon his bony nose. The man was so thin and frail, his skin so wrinkled and shrunken, that she felt she almost could see his bones.

". . . a certain work now entitled 'Knitting Book,' here-inafter called the Work," Rosenbloom read, then looked up at Marian. "I take it 'Knitting Book' is a working title."

"Yes," Marian nodded. "We haven't decided on a title as yet."

"I see. Actually, I can see no language in the contract per-taining to the title of the book. Whose province is it?"

"It's usually done by mutual consent. The author makes a title suggestion, and we either agree or disagree. It's never been a problem."

"Well, would you care if we inserted some language here, covering that more specifically? I'd like to see the words 'mutual consent' in the contract."

"All right," Marian acquiesced, "but as I say, it's never been a problem."

"There are few problems in drawing contracts, Mrs. Wall," Rosenbloom said, amusement showing in his eyes. "The problems arise when the contract is enforced."

"Exactly right," nodded Sam Beck, nudging Sadie with his elbow.

Rosenbloom read on through the next part of the contract, which dealt with Sadie's warranty that the work was original and did not violate anyone else's copyright. When he had finished, he looked at Sadie. "Do you understand all that, Sadie?" he asked. "Because the penalties in here are rather severe."

"I'm not so sure," Sadie said. "It sounded like a lot of Greek."

"You are guaranteeing to Harbor Press that the book is all yours."

"Of course," nodded Sadie.

"That all of your designs, or patterns, are yours alone and not copied from anyone else."

"Hey, wait a minute here!" Sadie said. "Who said I copied someone else? Every pattern I sent them is a Shapiro Original, thought up by me out of my own head. Listen, it was a long time ago when I stopped knitting from magazines and knitting books. What they're showing today, I was dreaming up maybe thirty years ago. So if anybody says I'm a copier, they're looking for trouble."

"I see," said Rosenbloom dryly, looking to Marian. "I would say we accept the warranty."

Rosenbloom continued through the contract for the next thirty minutes, and Marian found herself spellbound. The man's grasp of what must be to him an entirely alien field was amazing. As he explained each item to Sadie, taking legalese and rephrasing it in clear lay terms, she learned things about the Harbor Press contract she did not know were there. It was a brilliant performance.

At last Rosenbloom finished, apologizing to Marian for taking so much time. "I'm far from an expert on book contracts," he said, "although twenty years ago when Mr. Weymouth wrote his memoirs, I did make a thorough study of the field."

"You've remembered it well," said Marian.

"There is one last item that concerns me, though," said Rosenbloom. "I don't see it spelled out in the contract, and I'm a bit surprised. I'm thinking of commercial rights."

"I see," said Marian. She explained that a commercial-rights clause was only included in a Harbor Press contract when those rights were deemed valuable, and that in such cases the author and publisher split any monies received equally. "I don't think we have a problem here," she said, "do you?"

"Not offhand, no," said Rosenbloom, "but I hate leaving it up in the air. I don't think you ought to have commercial rights, in any case."

"Will one of you please tell me what's a commercial right?" Sadie asked.

"Manufactured items inspired by a book," said Rosenbloom.

"They could be anything," Marian said. "Mickey Mouse tee shirts is a good example. Or in your case, Sadie Shapiro tee shirts."

"My face on a tee shirt," Sadie grinned, "who would buy such a thing?"

"Me," said Sam Beck, keeping his face serious. "I would be the first customer for a Sadie Shapiro Tee Shirt."

"I think publishers should publish books, period," said Rosenbloom, ignoring him. "They have no right to exploit ideas or characters. Especially in this case. Sadie's face and personality belong only to herself. She is not a fictional character."

"I'm not so sure," said Sam Beck.

"If you have no objections, Mrs. Wall," Rosenbloom went on, "I'd like to insert a clause saying something like: 'All rights not herein granted to the publisher are reserved for the author.' I think that would nail it down. Is that agreeable?"

"I have no objections," said Marian, "but I'll have to check with Mr. Hawthorne. Is there a telephone nearby I could use?"

"This way," said Sam, showing Marian to the door. "Right down the hall." As she left, he turned to Rosenbloom. "You're doing a terrific job, Harold. I got to say you must have been a helluva lawyer in your time."

"In my time," Rosenbloom repeated, a strange half-smile on his face. Painfully, he drew himself to his feet and limped a few steps toward the door. "I'm really having great fun this afternoon," he said. "I hope I didn't drag it on too long."

"What drag?" said Sadie. "It was very interesting."

"My first legal work in eight years. Thanks for asking me, Sam. No one else has."

"I'll bet you really enjoyed your work, didn't you?" Sadie asked.

"Enjoyed it? It was my life, Sadie. The practice of law, the give-and-take, the hidden traps and sudden maneuvers. God, I miss it."

"If you don't mind my asking a personal question? How come, if you liked it so much, you decided to retire?"

Rosenbloom's laugh was humorless. "The tick of a clock did me in, Sadie, the turn of a page in a calendar. One day I was the head of a contract department of ten men—I was actually in the process of buying a large portion of north-western Brazil—and the next day I was sixty-five years old. Which meant I was out, finished, off the job. We had a mandatory retirement policy. The day you were sixty-five you walked out the door, even if you were God Himself. It's funny. I helped draft that policy when I first went to work for Weymouth and Lazard, forty years before. I thought then that when a man is sixty-five he should get out, to make room for the younger fellows. Who knew back then that I was hoisting myself on my own petard?"

Sadie shook her head in sympathy. "What's sixty-five? That's not any age at all. Sixty-five is a kid."

6

~~~~~~~~~~~~~~~~~

For Marian, it was proving to be a long summer. Three more gothic romances paraded across her desk that season, each one more dreadful than the last, and each one destined, of course, to set new sales records for Harbor Press. The ten-year-old air conditioning unit in her office window broke down, and it was only after weeks of fruitless complaining that repairs were begun. The result was a kind of warm sooty breeze that blew constantly on the back of her neck. Sweaty and harassed, she worked on through July and August, her red pencil crawling across endless pages of typescript describing endless moors and bleak country houses. On top of this there was the problem of Laura. Summer in New York is no festival for an eleven-year-old whose mother worked at the office at least forty hard hours a week and then brought manuscripts home on the weekend.

And Sadie Shapiro. Oh, God, and Sadie Shapiro.

The pride of Mount Eden called every day, sometimes twice a day. Now that the contract was signed, and Sadie was busily knitting sample garments to be photographed, it seemed that almost everyone at Mount Eden wanted to get in on the act. There were endless suggestions of new colors and new types of wool to be used for the garments. Every day Sadie would debate these choices with Marian over the phone, each conversation beginning with, "So how are you, darling Marian?" quickly followed by "So how is it going?"

The plain truth was it was going slowly. Much too slowly, in fact. Through the long hot summer Sadie had managed to knit only ten samples. Which, with the five already in Marian's hands, meant that there were still some thirty-five items her flying fingers must complete before all the photographs could be taken and the knitting book put to bed. To Marian, it seemed to take forever.

The slow pace was having its effect upon Arnold Hawthorne, too. More and more frequently Jack Gatewood would visit Marian's office, relaying the latest gossip he had heard at lunch. The list of publishers planning big knitting books was growing. There were at least five in the works now, perhaps more, and why can't you put some pressure on the old girl, Jack would say, so we don't get left at the starting gate?

Poor Jack, Marian thought, he was much too nice to be an editor-in-chief. Whenever he was called upon to criticize or apply pressure, his manner would grow ever more bluff, and the sports clichés would leap from his lips.

"Jack the jock," he was called by some others in the business, but Marian knew that the epithet was founded on envy. His rise in the business had been swift and sure. It had begun with one book, *Dribble to Glory,* the biography of a star professional basketball player who had been Jack's roommate at Ohio State. Once launched into the sports area, Jack had quickly turned himself into an editing-writing factory. Scores of athletes began to keep diaries, and he turned their almost illiterate products into fast-selling, highly promotable books.

But what about the real Jack Gatewood? After nine years of working side by side with Marian, he remained a mystery to her. Their relationship, so perfect in the office, ended with the close of the working day. And yet there had to be more to the man. Under his blazing virility and his actor's face, Marian felt certain, there was a part of himself Jack kept carefully hidden from view. More than once as she lay in

43

bed at night in the moments before sleep, Marian found herself thinking about Jack Gatewood.

It was on a Friday in late September that Sadie's slow progress brought on the crisis. Jack came into Marian's office, his face set, and sat down in the chair opposite her desk. "Prepare yourself for a shock," he began. "Arnold wants to back out of doing the knitting book."

"What!" was all Marian had time to say before Jack cut her off.

"I know," he nodded, "I've just spent an hour trying to talk him out of it, but his mind's made up. There are eight major publishers bringing out knitting books next fall. All the big boys are into it . . . Simon and Schuster, Random House, Doubleday. With competition like that, Mrs. Shapiro's book is overmatched."

"He can't do this!" Marian exploded. "You never know how a book will sell until you publish it. Sadie's book is different. It's . . ."

"Makes no difference," Jack said. "Arnold says if we don't publish the knitting book in the spring, forget it. And you know Arnold when he digs his heels in. Especially when he has cold feet."

"But we can't publish in the spring. There are still thirty-five samples to be completed."

"You can still make the spring list, Marian. I made Arnold give me that much. If you get hold of all the samples in two weeks, we can make it. We'd have to push on production, but we'd make it."

"Two weeks," Marian groaned, her heart turning over. "That's impossible, and Arnold knows it."

"I'm sorry," Jack said. "Truly I am."

"But it's dreadful, Jack. It will break Sadie's heart."

"We'll honor the contract, of course. She'll receive the rest of the advance."

"That's not the point," said Marian with some heat. "She's

an old woman. This book has become her whole life. To just drop the project so coldbloodedly . . . it's unfair, Jack."

"I wish I could help," said Jack. He avoided Marian's eyes and ran the toe of his Gucci slip-ons over the stained tile flooring in front of her desk.

"I'm going to speak to Arnold myself."

"You can't. He's left for the day, and he's taking a week's vacation. There's just no way he's going to change his mind."

"That's typical of Arnold," Marian said, "dropping something like this on me, and then running away."

"Just to make sure, he put it in writing, Marian. Unless the samples are in the house and ready for photography in two weeks, the book will be killed."

"The book is dead now, Jack. Thirty-five samples to be finished in two weeks . . . it can't be done."

"I'm sorry," Jack said, getting up from his chair. He stood there for a moment, his pale eyes fixed on Marian. "I never get the chance to bring you any good news, do I?" he said with a sad smile. "I guess you will have to break the news to her."

"Of course," Marian muttered through her teeth. "I get all the deadbeat assignments around here, don't I?"

His face once more a mask, Jack Gatewood retreated quickly, leaving a fuming Marian behind him. "Damn!" she exploded, banging one knee against her desk and tearing a hole in her $1.79 panty hose. How was she going to tell Sadie? And what would she do when the old woman broke down and cried?

She was still thinking about it when, two minutes later, the phone rang. "We are approaching Venice by moonlight," Heathcliff began. "Behind us, the gondolier is—"

"Not now!" said Marian. "I don't have time."

"But I never told you about Venice," said Heathcliff. "I have plans."

"I'm hanging up," said Marian, hanging up. She held a

trembling hand on the receiver for a moment, and then dialed Mount Eden. I'll just tell her, she reasoned. I'll jump right in there and tell her. And then she'll start crying, and I'll start crying and . . .

It took eight rings before Bertha Maloney answered, two minutes before she understood Marian's request, and a long five minutes before Sadie got to the phone. "Sit down, Sadie," Marian said, after exchanging greetings. "I have some very bad news."

"What's the matter," Sadie said. "You're not feeling well? Is Laura all right?"

"Laura is fine. It's about the book . . ."

"You lost the samples," Sadie said, "or you didn't get the latest batch I sent you—five pieces—the dirndl, the paisley shawl, one wide pleated skirt plus the two A-line shifts? Go ahead, trust the Post Office. My worst enemies could do a better job standing on one leg."

"Sadie," Marian interrupted, "it's not the samples. It's . . . the whole book."

"The whole book you lost? The patterns and everything?"

"I haven't lost anything, Sadie, but Arnold Hawthorne wants to back out of publishing the book. Sadie, if you don't have all the samples finished and in my hands in two weeks, there isn't going to be a book."

There was a long and chilling silence in which Marian's heart sank slowly into her sling-strap sandals. "Sadie? Are you there? Speak to me, Sadie . . . Hello?"

"Boy, oh boy, that's some little joke you just made there, Marian, if you don't mind my saying."

"Sadie, it's no joke. Two weeks, or Mr. Hawthorne insists we scrap the project. Things have happened. Lots of other publishers are bringing out similar books. We have to publish in the spring or not at all. I'm sorry to break it to you this way, but . . . Sadie? Hello?"

"I'm here, don't worry, I got no place to go. Tell your Mister Hawthorne, if I wasn't a lady, I'd say something that would make even me ashamed. Two weeks he gives me, to finish thirty samples," she said, sighing. "You get with a Simon Legree, what can you expect?"

"I know it's impossible—" Marian began.

"Who said impossible? Did I say impossible? Believe me, from this mouth you didn't hear that word."

"But Sadie, it *is* impossible. What Arnold is really saying is—"

"Two weeks he's saying, you don't have to tell me again. How do you like that no-goodnik? You start out with a man and all of a sudden he's making a sweatshop. Two weeks . . . and just when my arthritis is acting up, I can hardly move my pinky . . . two weeks."

"That's just it, Sadie. It can't be done and I don't want you killing yourself trying to do it."

"Hello," said Sadie, "how do you do?"

"Please, Sadie, it's only a book."

"Excuse me, Marian, but with me it's already a lot more than 'only a book.' It's my whole life. All right," said Sadie, "I don't need a singing telegram. Finish the job in two weeks, or it's goodbye, Charlie. That's it, right?"

"Yes . . . I'm sorry."

"Listen, if God could make the whole world in only one week and still get a day off besides, then maybe I can do the job also. What do you think, Marian?"

"I think I should send you the balance of your advance," Marian said slowly, "and I think you should take it—and not try to do the impossible. It's only going to hurt worse when you fail."

"Hey! Marian, whose side are you on? That's some terrific advice, I should pack up my knitting needles and go home."

"But, Sadie—"

"Never mind 'but Sadie.' Boy, if you were on that ship

with Columbus, Marian, we wouldn't be standing here in America today."

"You can't do it, Sadie."

"I *can* do it, Marian. A Shapiro never quits. Two weeks, the man says, and two weeks it'll have to be. If I have to work night and day, double-time and overtime. In fact, if you don't mind my saying, I shouldn't be standing here talking on the phone when every minute counts. So you'll excuse me, please."

"Wait!" Marian cried, "Sadie? . . ." But there was no reply. All Marian heard before the connection was broken was Sadie beginning to talk to herself. "Fingers," she was saying, "get ready to do your stuff."

7

~~~~~~~~~~~~~~~~~

"Oh my!" exclaimed Marian as she stepped into the taxi, "it's you again."

"You called the radio cab service, no?" said Juan Otero. He turned around to look at his passenger more closely.

"The Mount Eden Hotel in Queens? Remember?"

"Caramba!" said Juan Otero, "it is the lady who goes to see the jogging old woman." He surveyed Marian for a moment, looking especially at her hair. Some things never change, he thought. "We going to Hollis Avenue again?" he asked.

"For the last time, I think," said Marian as Juan put the clutch suddenly in gear and shot forward, forcing her back against the seat. The gloom of the day matched Marian's mood. Indeed, she could not remember having spent a worse two weeks. At home she snapped at Laura nearly every evening, and in the office things were more frantic than ever. She'd called Sadie every day, but the old woman had not deigned to come to the telephone. Only once, some three days ago, had she received any sort of reply. "Sadie says to tell you," the old switchboard operator had wheezed, "that a certain person is too busy to speak to another person when she is knitting her fingers to the bone, especially if that other person works for a slavedriver like Arnold Hawthorne, who shall be nameless."

Poor Sadie, Marian thought, as the taxi crawled along the expressway. She opened her handbag and looked at the check. The book was now officially dead and all that re-

49

mained was handing over the money and getting Sadie to take it.

"You a businesslady?" Juan called back from the front seat.

Marian nodded, and in reply to Juan's next question explained what she did. Juan nodded, impressed. "Editor," he said, "that is a fine job to have. Do I know some of your books, perhaps?"

"Have you read *Memoirs of a Painted Lady?*"

"No."

"*Hardcastle Castle?*"

"No."

Frowning, Marian reeled off twelve more popular titles until the taxi driver interrupted. "*Momento.* I know this Harbor Press. Do they not make a book called *Redecorating With Wallpaper?*"

Biting her lip ever so slightly, Marian nodded.

"Why did you not say that before?" Juan said expansively. "That is surely a famous book. In Puerto Rico it is a number-one best seller."

"I'm sure."

"You look on the highway outside Ponce, you see many tarpaper shacks covered with wallpaper now. Is a fine thing." With a squeal of brakes he pulled the taxi to a halt at Mount Eden's driveway. "Next time you call cab service, ask for Juan," he said as Marian stepped away from the cab and walked toward the ornate entranceway.

Unlike the way it was on her previous visits, Marian found no small crowd of Mount Edenites sitting under the porte-cochere as she strode toward the lobby. Nor were there any Mount Edenites visible inside. Where is everybody, Marian wondered as she made her way to the reception desk.

"Hellooo," came a voice from somewhere behind the counter. Bertha Maloney's aged gray head peeped out from behind the switchboard. "Aha, the editor lady herself, too!

of the sweatshop bosses. I suppose you're here to see Sadie."

Marian nodded, looking into unquestionably hostile eyes.

"For a handmaiden of the capitalist exploiters, I shouldn't do favors. But if you want Sadie, she's upstairs. Sixth floor, solarium."

"Well, thank you very much," Marian said icily. Turning on her heel, she strode briskly across the lobby. "Sixth floor," she said to the old elevator operator.

"I heard everything, you shouldn't be upset," he confided in a shaky whisper.

"What's got into that woman?" Marian asked.

The old man smiled grimly through yellowing teeth. "Commonist," he hissed. He put a spastic hand on the controls, and the car began to rise. "Over her bed, where ordinary people have a picture of their children, maybe a nice landscape?"

"Yes?"

"Karl Marx."

"Really?"

"Commonist."

Marian found herself nodding as the operator fixed his watery gaze on her, and nodding still more as the car jerked to a sudden stop and bounced up and down in place. "You want Shapiro, the fellow traveler, right? Down the hall to your left," he said, pointing a nicotine-stained finger.

Marian walked slowly down the corridor and approached a door marked "Solarium." As she came closer, she heard a strange clicking sound coming from within. Marian opened the door and stopped short, blinking at the strangest sight she had ever witnessed. Just about the total population of the Mount Eden Senior Citizens Hotel was gathered before her. There were seventy or eighty people, men and women, sitting in club chairs, deck chairs, bridge chairs and wheelchairs, all arranged in a rough circle. And every single one of them was knitting!

In the center of the circle, on her feet and talking a blue streak while knitting furiously, was Sadie Shapiro.

Marian didn't know whether to laugh or cry. Instead, she sank back against the wall to get her bearings.

"Terrific, Mendelson," Sadie was saying, "you go like that for three more rows. Smolowitz, I don't like the look of that loop you got there. Hold it! I'll be with you in a minute. Easy, Mr. Manfredi, you're going to bend the needle. Abe, wait for me, I'll show you how to do the next line. Fannie Johnson, *bubie*, rip that line out and do it over, if you'll be so kindly. Ipsy-pipsy, Bessie darling, I'll show you how to handle the cuff in two seconds!"

I don't believe it, thought Marian. This can't be happening.

"You're looking good, Mrs. Kanzer," Sadie was saying. "Keep going, Mr. Rosenbloom, you got a dozen more rows yet. A little bit more, Yetta, then I'll show you the other stitch. Courage, Meyer, you're doing terrific!" Turning to inspect the corps of knitters behind her, Sadie caught sight of her editor. "Marian!" She shrieked, "Marian, not yet! *The two weeks isn't up until tonight!*"

"*The publishing lady!*" an old woman in a wheelchair gasped. One by one, the crew of anxious knitters turned to look at Marian.

"*Too soon!*" called a man in a cardigan sweater, his hands continuing to knit the sleeve of a violet bolero jacket.

"*Go vay!*" called a heavyset woman working on a green shawl.

"*More time!*" cried a woman whose leg was in a plaster cast, and whose hands were just finishing the pom-pom of a wildly striped tam o'shanter.

"*We want more time!*" growled a bald-headed man working the sleeve of a maroon blazer. Others took up his cry. "We-want-more-time! We-want-more-time!" the Mount

Eden knitting brigade began to chant, stamping the floor with all the feet that were not confined to wheelchairs.

As the din mounted, Sadie came bounding across the solarium floor. "Not until tonight," she said desperately. "The two weeks isn't up until tonight!"

"We-want-more-time! We-want-more-time!" the chant went on.

"Please, Marian," Sadie pleaded, "a bargain is a bargain. By tonight you'll have it. Just give me till tonight."

"I'll have . . . what?"

"Everything!" Sadie said. "The whole shooting match in A-1 terrific shape."

"Everything?" Marian said, her eyes wide.

"When Sadie says everything, she means *everything*." There was a look of pride in Sadie's bright blue eyes. "Thirty samples, cookie, knitted and fitted and finished complete. In all the colors we agreed, in the exact sample sizes we need. Finished." A triumphant smile lit Sadie's face as Marian stared. "What do you think, Marian?"

"I think . . . I think I'm going to cry," Marian said.

"Now this," Sadie explained some time later as she led Marian into the physical therapy room, "this is the finishing room." She pointed to the dozen women who were busily stitching and basting and applying buttons and trim to a number of garments. Every exercise-table in the room, and there were at least a half-dozen, was covered with neatly knitted pieces. Here were two sleeves, a sweater front and a collar in shocking orange. There were the two halves of a pair of slacks being assembled by a grandmotherly type with pink hair. "Believe me," said Sadie, "it's what you call a regular bungalow industry."

"Cottage," said Marian.

"A crazy house, any way you look at it. Do I have to tell

53

you what's been doing here since you called me on the phone?"

"It's incredible, Sadie, fantastic. And you'll have everything done today?"

"By tonight, cookie, guaranteed. Every single sample. Just like Arnold Hawthorne, he should get a carbuncle on his big toe, said it had to be. Listen, where there's a will, there's a way out.

"The green piping goes on the yellow shawl, Mrs. Bloom!" she shouted, then shook her head in wonder. "Funny how sometimes you don't know about people. There I was, knitting my fingers off, knowing that no person in this world—especially one who's seventy-two or seventy-five years old—could possibly meet that deadline. And it turns out all I had to do was ask for help.

"I told Sam Beck and Bessie Frankel the spot I was in. Sam told Sarah Loeb, Bessie told Mr. Manfredi, he blabbed it around the dining room, and we were off to the races. Sarah brought in her bridge group, then the canasta people came in and the Mah-jongg Circle. The Great Books came around, and Sam and Abe Farkas brought the Men's Klaberjass and Pinochle Association. So all of a sudden I had ten, maybe twenty, experienced knitters and about sixty others just dying to help out. And then we got organized.

"Each good knitter took a hold of about ten of the others and showed them how to hold the needles, what to do, and like that. We laid out the patterns and instructions and divided up the work. The more experienced took the specialty items. The beginners we gave the easy things, the straight going.

"Sam took charge of the assembly line—he's a terrific organizer—he bought cold drinks for everyone, kept up morale, and provided the entertainment."

"Entertainment?"

"Singing, a few skits, nothing fancy. Listen, Harold Rosenbloom recites a poem, 'Trees,' could bring tears to your eyes. And meanwhile, Bessie got after the knitting store on Jamaica Avenue—a customer like me they don't get every day—and they started sending over the needles and the wool and the whatnot, and before you could say Jack-be-nimble, we were half-way finished. Believe me, Marian, it's been a wild and woolly two weeks around here."

Without quite knowing why, Marian found herself leaning over to kiss Sadie gently on the cheek. "Sadie," she said, smiling, "I actually do believe Harbor Press is going to be publishing a knitting book next spring."

Sadie nodded, her small face serious. "We got a big problem, though. You know up front in a book, where the writer says 'to my dear wife' or 'to my children'?"

"It's called the dedication page."

"Right. Well, on that page, Marian, I made a few promises. Do you think we can fit in about eighty names?"

Before Marian could answer, there was the sound of a commotion from the solarium. Sadie dashed to the connecting door with Marian close behind. Accompanied by a chorus of hoots and jeers, Max Adolphus was rapidly waddling across the crowded room, his round face flushed with anger. "What is the meaning of this?" he demanded of Sadie. "What's going on here?"

"What does it look like?" Sadie said blandly. "A few friends get together and knit a little bit, that's all."

"Come off it, Shapiro," the manager said. "This thing is organized, I can smell it. And if it's organized, it's unauthorized." Turning away he quickly scanned the crowd. "Mildred Futterman was due at her exercise class an hour ago, and so was Mr. Manfredi. And I see some people here who should be down in therapy. You're making trouble again, Shapiro," he said, whipping out a small black notebook from his breast pocket.

"But . . . isn't this therapy, of a sort?" Marian said.

55

"Who are you?" Adolphus asked, a belligerent look in his tiny eyes.

"She's my publisher," Sadie said.

"Editor," corrected Marian, who then introduced herself. "We're publishing Mrs. Shapiro's knitting book."

"A knitting book," Adolphus said slowly, "I see. That's also unauthorized, I might add." He jerked a butcherlike thumb at the knitting brigade. "And all these guests, here, they're helping out, I suppose?"

"Yes," Marian nodded. "They're knitting the sample garments we need for our photographs."

A sly grin creased the manager's round face. "Thank you very much," he said as he began to write in his notebook. "Conducting a business enterprise on the premises without permission is strictly against the rules. You know that, Shapiro. That's it, then. I'm putting you officially on notice. One more infraction, one more piece of trouble, and you are out of here, Shapiro. O-u-t, out." Slapping his notebook closed, the manager turned on his heel and stomped away.

"I'm sorry, Sadie," Marian said, as she watched the manager depart. "I guess I talked out of turn."

"Forget it, cookie," Sadie said, squeezing Marian's arm. "He had to find out anyway. And from that Omar the Tentmaker I'm not afraid."

"But, Sadie . . . suppose he does force you out of here? What would you do? Where would you go?"

"What will be, will be," Sadie shrugged. "Listen, you know what they say. You can't have an omelette without making eggs. Don't worry, a Shapiro will always get by."

"Forgive me," Marian began, but Sadie didn't hear.

"Wait, Mr. Schwartz, I'll help you turn the cuff!" she shouted, and in an instant she was away.

8

By now Marian knew that the woman who called herself Sadie Shapiro and dwelt in Mount Eden's somewhat tarnished splendor was something more than your average little old lady in tennis shoes. There was an elemental quality about Sadie, a life force that made things happen. It wasn't that she had godlike powers, or that the hand of the Almighty directed her actions. But it was just possible, Marian thought, that He dropped in on Sadie now and then and had a cup of tea.

The knitting book shaped up very quickly in the next few months, and production seemed to flow without a hitch. The photographs were clear and well-lighted; retouching was held to a minimum. The galley proofs were returned on time, a new record for Harbor Press. And even the art director supervising the layout, normally a flighty type much given to attacks of temperament, surprised everyone by turning out a first-rate job without making a fuss.

There was a hang-up over the title of the book, however.

Arnold Hawthorne had come up with a title suggested by Mrs. Hawthorne, and for a time he insisted that the book be called: *Knits—Neat and New!* Marian argued that this was off the track and Jack Gatewood agreed. Jack had a short list of rather uninspiring titles himself, the best of which (he thought) was *The NEW Knitting Book.* This presupposed, of course, that there was somewhere an old knitting book under the Harbor Press aegis, which was not the case.

Marian found herself at odd moments scribbling possible titles on the backs of envelopes and in the margins of other manuscripts. She even took the well-thumbed Roget's *Thesaurus* from behind the desk at home and scoured the categories of superlatives.

Sadie, of course, knew all along what the title of her knitting book would be. As she told Marian over the telephone one day when the title search had reached the proportions of a major crisis, "Darling, stop fooling around with crazy titles for my book. The name of the book is going to be *Sadie Shapiro's Knitting Book* by Sadie Shapiro, and that's it. Not because I got a swell head and I want to see my name on a book, although God knows when I finally do see this book, I'll probably jump in the air and do a few ballet steps on the way down. But because, look, my name happens to be Sadie Shapiro and this is a knitting book written by me, so it's only logical, right? And besides, there probably hasn't been another woman named Sadie Shapiro who ever wrote a knitting book, so no one would ever confuse it, either. Am I making myself clear?"

"Perfectly," said Marian. A few moments later she was trying it out on Jack Gatewood.

"It just won't do," he said, swiveling in his big black leather chair, his fingertips tented at his chest.

"Why not?" asked Marian.

"Well," Jack began, "it . . . ahh . . . mmm."

Sensing doubt, Marian plunged ahead. "Don't dismiss it, Jack. Try it. Go ahead, repeat it to yourself a few times."

"That's silly, Marian."

"Sadie Shapiro's Knitting Book," Jack said. "Ridiculous." And yet, even as he dismissed it, a smile played at the corner of his lips. *"Sadie Shapiro's Knitting Book,"* he said very slowly.

"You see?"

A grin crossed Gatewood's actor's face. "It does have a ring to it. *Sadie Shapiro's Knitting Book* . . ."

"The title of the year."

"*Sadie Shapiro's Knitting Book*." Jack laughed. "I'll be damned," he said, "now you've got me liking it, too." He stood up and smiled. "Come," he said, "we're off to see the wizard."

"You're crazy," said Arnold Hawthorne. "It's just unheard of."

"*Sadie Shapiro's Knitting Book*," Jack said, pacing before Hawthorne's desk.

"Insanity," Hawthorne said. "You've both been drinking."

"*Sadie Shapiro's Knitting Book*," Marian said. "Try it, you'll like it."

"It's like a mystic incantation," Jack said. "Go ahead, Arnold, say it."

"*Sadie Shapiro's Knitting Book*," Marian said.

"*Sadie Shapiro's Knitting Book*," the publisher said.

"Say it again," Marian insisted.

"*Sadie Shapiro's Knitting Book*," Hawthorne said, more slowly this time. "*Sadie Shapiro's Knitting Book?*"

"Exactly," said Jack.

"Incomprehensible," said Arnold Hawthorne. "And yet . . . *Sadie Shapiro's Knitting Book* . . ."

"He's hooked," Marian said.

A dazed smile crossed the heavyset publisher's face. "*Sadie Shapiro's Knitting Book!*"

"You see?" Jack said, pointing a finger. "That's what happened to me. It's very hard to hate a title like that."

"Done, and done," said Arnold Hawthorne, shaking hands with himself. "And whose brainstorm is it?" he asked Marian.

"Who else?" she said, raising her shoulders in a shrugging gesture that was unaccustomed, and yet oddly familiar.

9

~~~~~~~~~~~~~~~~

The day Sadie Shapiro's book was officially published dawned bright and clear. The sun lifted the fog over Jamaica Bay, disregarded the stench of decaying fish, and rose in the polluted gray sky to warm the city. For the people at Harbor Press, and for Sadie Shapiro, it was Publication Day, a time of joy and hope, and simple but dignified ceremony.

Ask any author about Publication Day, as it's commonly called, and he will probably recall with utmost clarity the dreams and aspirations expressed to him on that day by his editor and the others associated with his book. But Pub Day means more than that, for it is the day upon which the book in question is officially offered for sale in all the bookshops of the nation. No matter that half the bookshops have probably not received the work, and the other half have chosen to display it in some dark corner of the store behind a post. And so as Marian Wall sat in her cramped office awaiting Sadie's arrival, she pushed aside the gray nubbins of failure already associated with the book. She did not dwell upon the four book clubs that had recently rejected it, nor the fact that it had been overlooked by the trade journal, *Publishers Weekly*. For it was publication day, and failure had no place at the table.

At the appointed lunchtime hour, Sadie arrived, her face aglow with excitement. She was wearing a shiny black satin dress with a corsage of gardenias pinned at the shoulder. These were a gift from Sam Beck, who had seen her safely into a taxi. Sadie looked absolutely lovely, at least to Marian, and the two women fell upon each other and exchanged warm hugs. Then Marian led Sadie on a short tour of Harbor Press, ending in the office of the publisher.

"This is our editor-in-chief, Mr. Gatewood," said Marian.

"Call me Jack," said Jack, extending his hand.

Sadie stopped and stared, putting a bony hand to her chest. "A Greek god," she said, "a Hollywood actor. I can't believe that he can also be an editor-in-chief."

"Yes . . . well," Gatewood mumbled as the color rose in his cheeks.

Sadie nudged Marian gently. "So handsome," she stage-whispered, pursing her lips. "Why didn't you tell me hand-some, Marian?"

At this awkward moment Arnold Hawthorne, stepping carefully over the bare spot in his carpet, came forward and shook Sadie's hand. "Lovely," he said, beaming. "I've looked forward to this moment for many months."

Sadie tore her gaze away from Jack Gatewood's face and turned to greet her publisher. "So you're the famous Arnold Hawthorne," she said, leaning backward as if to get a better view. "Not bad," she nodded. "You look a little bit like my Reuben, may God let him rest, except, of course, my Reuben wasn't as bald as you are, Mr. Hawthorne, and he was maybe a good twenty pounds lighter."

"I see . . . yes," Hawthorne grinned weakly, the color in his face rising to match Jack Gatewood's.

"Cake and bread," Sadie said, nodding sagely.

"Yes?"

"Deadly enemies. Believe me, a piece of cake will kill you faster than anything. And bread . . . with you that's an old story already." She poked a gentle index finger at Haw-thorne's belt line and then brought it up to shake at him. "I'll bet you're a naughty boy at the dinner table, right?"

In the silence that followed, Jack Gatewood managed to

clear his throat. "Speaking of food," he said weakly, "how about lunch?"

"I thought you'd never ask," Marian whispered. Grabbing Sadie's arm, she whisked her away down the hall. As they waited for Jack to retrieve his hat, Sadie surveyed the small waiting room that faced the elevators.

"So this is publishing," she mused aloud, noting the balls of dust under the receptionist's desk and the strange off-gray paint that peeled from the walls. "Reminds me a little of my brother-in-law's place."

"Is he in publishing?"

"Millinery."

Downstairs as they stepped out into bright sunshine, Jack began searching for the taxi he had telephoned for. "We always buy our authors a good-luck lunch on publication day." He smiled at Sadie.

The cab pulled in at the curb. *"Buenos dias,* publishing lady," the driver called.

"Do you know him?" a puzzled Jack Gatewood asked, as he helped Sadie and Marian climb inside.

"We get lost together in Queens now and then," Marian said.

"Hey," Juan Otero exclaimed, turning around to look at Sadie, "it is the lady who jogs. *Por favor,* I did not recognize you without your sweat suit."

"Hello, cabman," said Sadie.

"Your book," said Juan, "how does it go?"

"Published today. Right this very minute, I want you to know, you are actually speaking to an author."

"Felicidad," said Juan, flashing a golden smile. "May your book have all the success of *Redecorating With Wallpaper."*

"What's going on here?" Jack whispered to Marian.

"It's a long story," she said. "To the Tuscan Pavilion, Juan, whenever you get around to it."

The journey to the restaurant, crosstown at the noon hour,

62

took twenty minutes. Added to that, of course, was the five minutes required to say goodbye to Juan Otero.

"Good afternoon, Mr. Gatewood," said Pietro, the maître d'. "I have a table for three overlooking the garden." With a sweeping half-bow, Pietro led the trio down the steps of the vestibule and into the elegant restaurant. Sadie's eyes were everywhere as she followed. "Look at this!" she exclaimed, pointing to the hors d'oeuvre table. "A whole big piece of lox!"

"Smoked salmon, madame," Pietro corrected.

"Nova Scotia?"

"Scotch."

"Amazing," said Sadie. "I didn't even know they had lox over there. And what's this?" she added, pointing a pink-tipped finger.

"That, madame, is smoked eel. Caught three days ago at Montauk Point and smoked for forty-eight hours in our own smoke oven."

Sadie's mouth dropped open and just as quickly closed. "Don't show me any more things," she said, "not if I'm going to eat."

Their table sparkled with glassware and snowy white napery. "Now then," said Jack when they were seated, "what shall we have to drink? Sadie?"

"Water will be fine. I'm not a drinking person."

"Come now, it's publication day. I think a small celebration would be in order."

"All right," said Sadie, "I'll take a chance. What the heck, I could be dead any minute, anyway. But nothing strong, please."

"Excellent," smiled Jack. He beckoned to the hovering waiter and ordered Marian's usual Scotch and a light aperitif for Sadie. "And bring me a Beefeater martini, extra dry, stand up, twist of lemon." Jack looked at Sadie. "Better make that last a double," he added.

When the drinks arrived, Jack raised his glass. "To *Sadie Shapiro's Knitting Book* and the charming lady of the title."

Sadie smiled, waited while the others drank, then ventured a sip of her own libation. She smacked her lips. "Not Manischewitz Concord," she said, "but not too terrible either." She took another sip. "In fact, if I really tried, I might even like it."

Pietro quietly materialized and handed round the enormous menus.

"I could eat a horse," said Sadie. "I only had a bowl of Wheaties for breakfast."

"May I suggest the *moules vinaigrette* as an appetizer?" Pietro said. Marian and Jack nodded assent.

"What is this?" Sadie asked, her finger held firmly on the menu.

"Prosciutto and melon, madame," said Pietro in his suavest manner. "We take the smoked Parma ham, slightly peppered and sliced in thin strips and wind it lovingly over slices of ripe Persian melon. Would madame care to try it?"

"Of course, but without the ham and pepper, please."

Pietro made the notation on his pad without the slightest hesitation. "And for the main course, madame, I would suggest the *vitello tonnato*. Which is a braised loin of milk-fed veal, with a light tuna-fish sauce." He kissed his fingertips. "Today, it is for the gods."

"Sold," said Marian.

"Me, too," said Jack.

"Tuna-fish sauce," Sadie said, shivering, "you know what this is to a gall bladder?"

"The madame has a *problème digestif?*" said Pietro. "I sympathize."

"It's the old story," said Sadie, holding a hand to her right breast. "Your eyes and your mouth are what kills your whole body."

"How true," said Pietro. "I, too, suffer from this complaint."

"Is that right?" said Sadie. "A young man like you with a gall bladder?"

"Since two years now."

"You eat something a little fatty, and it's like a hot hand grabbing you inside."

"Exactement."

"Try a little cole slaw, you might as well make out your will."

"Ah, yes, you know it well. Just yesterday, I ventured only a tiny mouthful—the merest trifle—of *boeuf à la mode*."

"Shame on you."

"Indeed. Half the night I could not sleep."

"Ay-yi-yi," clucked Sadie. "You took your Gelusil?"

"It did not help."

"A hot cup of tea, maybe?"

"Nothing helped."

"I usually try to sleep sitting up. You ever try that? Take two pillows and lay back kind of sitting up?"

"Interesting," said Pietro. "It sounds like it may be a good idea."

"Couldn't hurt."

"I often find a heating pad to be of some small comfort."

"Or a hot water bottle."

"And, of course, just standing will help to relieve the pressure."

"A short walk in the fresh air."

"On the West Side of Manhattan, one does not often go walking late at night. Of course, that might end one's gallbladder problems permanently."

"Right," said Sadie with a smile. "So I don't have to tell you what to bring me."

"Leave it to me," said Pietro. "I will bring you what I have set aside for my own luncheon." With a graceful half-bow, he turned and glided away.

"I don't believe it," said Jack, after a short silence. He stared at the retreating Pietro. "Five years I've been eating lunch here, and the most he's ever said to me is 'Nice weather we're having.'"

"Listen," said Sadie, breaking the edge off a crusty roll, "you just have to know how to talk to people."

10

~~~~~~~~~~~~~

"How dare you burst into my laboratory this way!" Philip Sidney, Third Earl of Worcestershire, demanded. He stood before Marian, barring further entry into the dimly lit chamber, his rounded lips set in a hard line that displayed his strong jaw to full advantage. "Get out, you little fool," he said, "before you see too much."

"I must know, Philip," Marian said in a voice that trembled. "They are saying . . . in the village . . . that you . . ."

Philip Sidney laughed. "I am well aware what those fools think. And you believe it, don't you?"

"But the practice of alchemy, Philip, is expressly forbidden by—"

"Alchemy, is it?" the Third Earl said curtly. He strode toward his laboratory table and turned to face the beautiful young governess.

"Wa-wa?" said Marian Wall, as the ringing telephone cut short her dream. Blinking sleep from her eyes, she fielded the receiver on the third ring.

"We are standing atop the Eiffel Tower, my darling," Heathcliff began. "It is dawn, and below us the City of Light is at your feet."

"What time is it?"

"I told you—it is dawn."

"I mean now."

"Oh," said Heathcliff. "Ten after seven."

"Yipes! I've overslept!"

"Hey, wait a minute. Marian! We're in Paris, see—"

"Thanks for waking me. Talk to you later." She put the telephone down and swung her legs off the bed.

Walking slowly, she paused for a look in the bedroom mirror before going into the bathroom. My hair, she thought, I must do something with my hair. Like hack it all off and start again. A sudden burst of cacophony from the kitchen told her that Laura was up and about. Moving like a sleepwalker, Marian shuffled off to the shower.

A flurry of shouts, grunts, pistol shots and clanging gongs greeted her some moments later as she joined Laura in the kitchen. "Turn the radio down," Marian said. "I can't stand that awful racket before coffee."

"Aw, Ma, that's super-dooper hit-one-hit-one," Laura said.

"My God, you're beginning to talk like that rock station you're always listening to."

"Shhh!" Laura shushed. "It's my favorite."

Marian turned away and busied herself with the breakfast ritual. She opened the cabinet and took down the seven bottles of vitamins and minerals that supplemented her unbalanced diet. She quickly gobbled a Vitamin C, two E's, a multi-vitamin with iron, another with niacin, several wheat-germ-oil tablets and a Unicap for good measure. Pouring a glass of orange juice, she stood for a moment, her back against the refrigerator, and surveyed her daughter. Laura came within twenty pounds of being beautiful, Marian thought, and a diet was definitely in order. The girl's eyes were almond-shaped and huge, when she didn't scrunch them up, and the rest of her features were finely shaped. But all of this was hidden by the problem of her weight. You saw her round cheeks first and her rounded figure next. There was something sick about the way Laura attacked food.

"What are you doing?" she asked, as the child busied herself at the table.

"Flying an airplane," Laura said, sighing a little and fluttering her eyelashes at the ceiling.

"Laura," Marian said, a cautioning tone creeping into her voice.

"Oh, Mom!" Laura exploded, "I've got a butter knife in one hand and a doughnut in the other. What the hell do you think I'm doing? I'm buttering a doughnut."

"See here, young lady," Marian countered, "don't speak to me that way."

"When I hear a stupid question, I give a stupid answer," Laura said. She took a snapping bite of the doughnut in her hand. "I'm sorry, it must be the way I've been brought up." She exchanged a high-velocity glare with her mother.

Marian looked briefly into Laura's eyes and found she could not quite bear to see the girl's animus reflected so nakedly. She turned away and covered her emotion by searching for the instant coffee in the cabinet. Does every mother argue with her daughter, she wondered, or am I the only one? In any case, the communications problem had become acute. Trying to keep her voice under control, she began again. "Did you do your homework?"

"Yes," said Laura, with a tragic sigh.

"Do you need any pocket money?"

"No."

Marian drew a pot of water and set it on the stove to heat. Turning to Laura again, she asked, "Why do we have trouble talking?"

"I don't know," Laura said. Her finger was making small designs on the dusty table. "Maybe I need a father."

"You had one," Marian said. "It didn't work out."

"Maybe *you* need something, then."

Right in the heart, thought Marian. "Maybe," she said, shrugging. "If you find out what it is, let me know."

Laura downed the rest of her milk in one swift swallow and went off to collect her school books. A few moments

69

later, when she pecked Marian on the cheek before leaving, her lips seemed to be made of ice.

The anger of the morning stayed with her as Marian dressed and fought her way across Manhattan to the office. The morning commute, always on a level just short of physical combat, was more irritating than usual. There were more candy wrappers per square yard on the street. A greater quotient of *Angst* and *Weltschmerz* was written on the faces of the people standing about her in the bus. And the Grindl Building, never an architectural marvel on the best of days, seemed somehow grimier and even more forlorn than ever today.

The monthly sales figures that were waiting on her desk did not improve Marian's mood. The knitting book was not doing well. Just a month after publication, and after the two small ads had run in support, Harbor Press had shipped less than two thousand copies. For a project as costly as Sadie's, it was just short of disaster, and much less than the optimistic forecast prepared by the sales department. Damn and double damn, thought Marian. She took the container of black coffee she had bought downstairs and gently prised off the lid, managing to spill only a few drops on the computer printout sheet that held the sales figures. *Hardcastle Castle* was selling well at least, and so was the new southern-style gothic. But topping the list, as it had ever since publication two years before, was the redoubtable *Redecorating With Wallpaper*.

With a few lucky breaks, Sadie's book might be up there, too. Something had to be done before the book simply fell into oblivion. Sales figures in hand, she hurried off to Arnold Hawthorne's office. "Arnold," she said, seating herself next to his desk, "I demand a promotion!"

A look of pain crossed the publisher's face. "Look, Marian," he said quickly, "business is awful, sales are down. I know you're expecting a raise, but the way things are—"

70

"Not me. The book. Sadie's book."

"I saw the figures," said Hawthorne, rolling his eyes. "Dying on the vine, from the look of it."

"A poor start," Marian corrected, "but the potential is there . . . *if* we help it happen."

"Oh, well," Hawthorne said, "we've already run two big ads."

"A sixteenth of a page each."

"Which is what the budget will allow," said Hawthorne. He shook his head. "I won't throw good money after bad, Marian. Maybe, in a month or two, if the figures look good, we'll think about another ad."

"Which will be another sixteenth of a page and won't help at all." Now it was Marian's turn to look pained. "Arnold, don't you see? A little money spent right now is what's needed. And some kind of promotion, aside from ads. Like it or not, Sadie's book is unique. Those little mittens with the animal faces on them, and that paisley shift dress . . . no one has ever seen anything like them. Somewhere there's a feature article for the women's magazines, I can feel it in my bones."

"I agree," said Hawthorne, "but we seem to be overlooked when it comes to publicity. Harbor Press is a small outfit. We can't afford a giant staff of full-time publicity people."

"How about one?"

Hawthorne's face reddened and he drew himself up in his chair. "We do have publicity representation, as you very well know, Marian. It's just that . . . well, my wife has been busy lately, what with opening the summer house and our daughter getting married, and she can't handle the job as she used to.

"By the way," he added, neatly shifting gears, "have you seen the new sales figures on *Redecorating With Wallpaper?*"

Across town, at that very moment, the problem of promoting Sadie's book was also under consideration. Seated at a sunny table in Mount Eden's back garden, the author listened closely as Sam Beck held forth. "They're not doing enough, Sadie, not by half. I'm telling you, a book like yours should be selling like pancakes."

"But what more can they do?" said Sadie. "They already put two ads in the paper."

"They were very nice ads, too," said Bessie Frankel. "I was so proud to see them, I even called my daughters about it."

"They were piffle," Sam Beck said scornfully. "Little nothings, the both of them. If you looked fast you were sure to miss them. That's not the way to advertise a book. Believe me, I know. I used to be in the advertising business."

"I didn't know that," Sadie said.

"Matchbook covers," Beck said proudly.

"Sam's right," Harold Rosenbloom said, breaking his usual silence. "I'm sorry, Sadie, I should have thought of it earlier," he went on. "I did have considerable experience in promoting Mr. Weymouth's memoirs, with very little result, I might add. Nonetheless, I do think that Harbor Press has been very lax. Perhaps we should have insisted on a promotion budget before you signed your contract."

"Please, Harold," said Sadie, shaking her head. "I'm just so glad they published the book, who could ask for more? I mean, just to see that book with my name on it and all my patterns in it is enough. What do I care if it's a big seller?"

"Nonsense," scoffed Sam Beck. "If you do a thing, do it right. I think your book is terrific. I think everybody should be reading it."

"Right," said Abe Farkas, "no home should be without one."

"Thanks a lot," Sadie smiled, "but don't get crazy. I mean, it's a knitting book, not a Bible. For people who knit."

72

"Wrong," Beck countered. "All wrong. Listen, I have your book right on my night table. And every night I read a little before I go to bed."

"You read what?" Sadie asked. "It's all instructions, Sam. A lot of numbers."

"Is that right? Well, last night I happened to be reading all about making that paisley shift dress. I thought it was very interesting."

"Put him right to sleep," Farkas said.

"Let's get back to promotion," Harold Rosenbloom said. "I think we ought to pool our collective brains and consider the problem. Surely, between us we have some contacts who might prove useful. Think."

"I am thinking," Beck said, "but nothing's happening."

"Excuse me," Bessie Frankel said, but Beck interrupted her. "Twenty-five years I belonged to the Knights of Pythias. Each year they have a few meetings when the wives come down. Maybe I could fix it up so Sadie could give a knitting talk at the next wives' night."

"All right," Rosenbloom said, "that's a start." He took a gold pen from his breast pocket and began making notes on a table napkin.

"Excuse me," Bessie said.

"Excuse me, Bessie," Abe Farkas cut in. "Dry goods stores I used to have, but now my son is running them. I mean, we never sold books in our stores before, but for Sadie we could make an exception. We could make a window display and everything."

"A little off the track," Rosenbloom said, "but you've given me an idea. Aren't there a lot of knitting stores in the country?"

"Of course," Sadie said. "There are three on Jamaica Avenue alone."

"Well, they ought to be selling your book," said Rosen-

73

bloom. "People who frequent knitting stores obviously must be knitters. And that's your market, Sadie."

"Excuse me," said Bessie, but Beck interrupted. "And how about department stores? They not only sell books, but they have knitting departments."

"Right," Rosenbloom nodded, "a perfect spot for a tie-in promotion. Very good, Sam. Now we have to start thinking of how the promotion should be handled." He sat back in his chair and removed his eyeglasses, rubbing the bridge of his nose with his fingertips. "A promotion," he said. "What would make a good promotion?" There was a moment's silence as Rosenbloom led the group in concentration.

"Excuse me," Bessie Frankel said for the fourth time. With no one to interrupt, she went on. "My son-in-law, Myron, a wart should grow on his earlobe for putting me here, could maybe help. I think."

"What does he do, sell books?" Farkas asked.

"No. No, he doesn't sell books," Bessie said.

"He buys books, then," Sam Beck said.

"No," said Bessie, "Myron doesn't buy books."

"Well," said Sam, "he doesn't buy or sell books. That's clear. Are you going to tell us what he does, Bessie, or do we have to guess?"

Bessie hesitated, moving her head from side to side. "I mean, I'm not too sure about his job. We haven't said a word to each other in six months . . ." Again, Bessie hesitated.

"And?" Beck said impatiently.

"Don't mix me up, Sam," Bessie said. "I'm trying to think. I remember, a long time ago, Myron once said something about being an *interviewer*. Is that the right word? Someone who talks to people?"

"That's the word," said Harold Rosenbloom.

"Terrific," Abe Farkas snorted. "What's he in, personnel work?"

"No," said Bessie, "not that. Let me think . . ."

74

"He's a milkman, mark my words," Farkas said.

"Wait a minute," Bessie said, a smile breaking out, "now I got it. Yes, sure, I remember now. It's a program, late at night, but I don't stay up that late, and I don't watch television anyway . . ."

The mention of that magic word brought the others up short. It seemed an eternity before Bessie went on. "Right," she said, nodding to herself, "he's an interviewer, my Rosalie's Myron, that's what he does. He picks out the people who go on this program, and he talks to them before. In fact, I think he said he's in charge of it."

"A television show?" Rosenbloom said slowly.

"Right. On NBC . . . with a Johnny somebody on it . . ."

"Carson?"

"Oh, you know it?" said Bessie. "Right. What Myron does is pick out the people who go on that Johnny Carson show. In fact, I just got a letter. He and my Rosalie are coming in from California. They're going to be doing that program in New York for a few weeks. Do you think it would help if I asked Myron to put Sadie on?"

11

~~~~~~~~~~~~~~~

Johnny Carson's Green Room is actually painted a deep shade of blue and is kept at a cool 72° F. Her hair neatly combed and lacquered, her face smoothed by layers of deep tan pancake makeup, Sadie Shapiro sat quietly in a club chair next to Marian while three young production assistants hovered nearby in a state of constant attention. To Marian's wondering eyes, Sadie was easily the calmest person in the room. In fact, she had maintained that calm through all the excitement of two pre-show interviews and the subsequent preparations for her appearance.

"Thirty seconds to tape," a voice announced, and the three assistants nodded at one another. Sadie winked at them.

"You know what to say?" Marian asked.

Sadie nodded. "Mr. Carson will ask me questions, and I'll answer them."

"Right. And then what?"

"Then he'll ask me to knit, and I'll do a few lines, and then I ask him if he wants to try it, and I pass him the needles, and he'll try it and get all mixed up, and it'll be funny."

"Perfect," Marian said. "Just remember, speak slowly and don't be nervous."

Sadie patted Marian's arm. "What have I got to worry?" she said, the corners of her eyes crinkling. "They're going to kill me if I don't make a hit?"

"That's the spirit," Marian said, keeping her voice merry. "You'll do fine."

The two women settled back and gave their attention to

the large color TV set in front of them. The Tonight Show had just begun, and Ed McMahon was running through the guest list: Mel Brooks, Joe Namath and Sarah Vaughan. Sadie's name, of course, was last, and was the only one not spelled out in white letters on the screen.

The New York Jets football star, Joe Namath, fresh from the makeup room, came walking into the room just as Carson was introduced and began his monologue. He nodded at Marian and Sadie and settled down on a couch nearby. In a few minutes, as Carson wound up his monologue and hit a practice golf shot at the band, Mel Brooks came in. Right behind him came the Tonight Show's assistant producer. He squatted down in front of Sadie and Marian. "Mrs. Shapiro," he said, "there's been a change of scheduling. Instead of putting you on last, Johnny wants you first. That way you can do your bit with him, we'll cut away for a station break at the hour, and you can leave."

"All right," Sadie said, her eyes on the big TV set, watching a beer commercial.

The producer got to his feet. "Karnak is on next," he said. "When he's about finished, we'll get you ready outside, and you'll be on after the commercial break . . ."

"Whatever," said Sadie.

"And now," McMahon was saying on the tube, "here he is. The soothsayer of the East, the magical mind that mystifies many millions from Manhattan to Mandalay, and also a leader in the rented tuxedo field . . . *KARNAK!* The Magnificent!"

"He's sometimes very funny," Marian said.

"I never saw him," said Sadie.

Carson/Karnak entered, draped in a cape and wearing his ridiculous swami turban, and, of course, managed to trip over the platform on the way to his seat.

"In these envelopes," McMahon was saying, "which have been hermetically sealed and left in a mayonnaise jar on

77

Funk and Wagnall's back porch, are many questions. Karnak the Magnificent will first tell us the correct answer, and then open each envelope to read the question." McMahon smiled. "Are you ready, O Magnificent One?"

"May the great bird of Paradise drop a doo-doo on your beanie," Karnak answered, his turban askew. He took the first envelope from McMahon and pressed it to his temple.

"What is he doing?" Sadie asked.

"It's a bit," Marian said. "A shtick."

"A shtick what?"

"And the first answer?" McMahon intoned.

Karnak's eyebrows began doing push-ups. "Philip the Third," he said.

"Philip the Third!" McMahon shouted in echo as Karnak's turban flew off. Carson blew open the envelope and read from the card inside: "What do you do when you've downed two glasses of bicarbonate, and you've still got a pizza heartburn?"

"Oooh," said McMahon with a pained look.

"Great Karnak have heartburn after that one," Carson said.

"Marian, he's sick?" Sadie asked. She looked genuinely puzzled.

"It's supposed to be funny," Marian said, as two of the production assistants shot her dark looks.

McMahon handed Karnak the next envelope, but their ensuing lines were drowned out by a gust of laughter from the other guests on the couch. Sadie turned to them. "Sha!" she commanded. "We're trying to watch a program here, if you'll be so kind."

Marian blanched at Sadie's outburst and sank down in her chair. But the guests on the couch merely smiled.

The assistant producer entered and conducted Sadie and Marian from the Green Room and into the wings as Karnak's bit came to a close. A makeup man shot a last spray of lacquer at Sadie's gray hair, the assistant producer whispered, "Smile," and then, with a cheery wave, Sadie walked toward the curtain as Carson wound up her introduction.

". . . the author of *Sadie Shapiro's Knitting Book,* one of the world's best knitting instructors, won't you greet Mrs. Sadie Shapiro."

As the applause rose and Sadie emerged from behind the curtain into the lights, Marian found that her fingertips were in her mouth. She looked at the monitor set just backstage to see what the world was seeing: an elderly gray-haired woman, slim, small, and rather spry, her face set in a wide smile, carrying a "Jamaica Avenue Knittery" shopping bag and walking very slowly toward the Tonight Show set. Marian took her fingers from her mouth and crossed them.

Johnny Carson, standing politely, shook Sadie's hand as she seated herself in the guest's chair. "Well now," Carson said as McMahon sat down and the applause died, "I don't think we've ever had a knitting instructor on with us before . . ."

Sadie turned to grin at Bessie Frankel, who was seated in the audience along with Sam Beck, and then turned back to the host.

". . . but your book is so unusual, we decided to have you on." He smiled at Sadie, who smiled right back. But she didn't say anything, and for a moment she was in full close-up, a grin set on her face.

"Scared out of her mind," the assistant producer whispered to Marian. "She'd better not freeze out there."

Carson picked up a copy of the knitting book as the camera zoomed in close. *"Sadie Shapiro's Knitting Book* is the title of Mrs. Shapiro's book—I guess that's appropriate—and it's published by Harbor Press," Carson said. "I understand it's selling very well."

The camera swung to Sadie who nodded once, the smile gone.

"Oh, God!" the producer moaned to Marian.

"Yes, indeedy," Carson grinned, as if to himself, "that's what they say . . ." A look of impending disaster could be seen in his eyes. "Well, now . . . ah . . . Mrs. Shapiro . . . I hear that you may actually be the world's most experienced knitter. How long, actually, has it been since you first began playing with needles?"

There was an enormous close-up of Sadie, who looked at the ceiling and sat back in the chair, thinking. "I started," she said, pausing, "I think when I was carrying Stuart . . ."

"Stuart?" Carson broke in.

". . . and I wanted to make a pair of booties, you know—they didn't have them like they have them today—I mean, just to walk in and buy . . ."

"Yes?"

"So it means, wait a minute, it's like . . . maybe fifty-one, fifty-two years already . . . easy."

"I see," said Carson, his hand fiddling with the leading edge of his tie. "Stuart, I take it, is your son."

"Correct."

"And you began knitting as a hobby when you were pregnant . . ."

Sadie's mouth dropped open, and she looked genuinely shocked. "Oooh," she said, "like that you talk on television?"

There was a shot of Carson's surprised face as a few people in the audience tittered. Carson looked behind him, as if to say: Who, me? "I'm sorry," he grinned. "What did I say?"

Sadie's face was serious. "I wouldn't repeat it."

"Oh," said Carson, "you mean 'pregnant'?"

"Ayee, you said it again!" cried Sadie, provoking a gust of laughter.

"Listen," she added, "in my day we didn't talk like that. I mean, you could say a woman was 'that way,' or maybe 'expecting,' but a word like you used we wouldn't even say in the parlor, not to mention on TV."

"*Well,*" said Carson in his Jack Benny voice, "I won't mention it again, Mrs. Shapiro. By the way, may I call you Sadie?"

"Of course. And I'll call you Mr. Carson."

There was a light in Sadie's eyes as she grinned slyly at Johnny, and backstage Marian could see that Sadie was beginning to relax. "The old lady's coming on," the assistant producer said.

"Do you mind, Sadie, if I ask how old you are?"

"Of course I mind," Sadie began, getting a laugh, "but I'll tell you anyway. This year, God willing, I'll be seventy-two . . ."

There was instant and loud applause with Carson leading it. When it died down, Sadie added: ". . . or seventy-five years old." She knocked wood on the desk as the audience laughed wildly. Ed McMahon, sitting next to Sadie, doubled over with laughter.

"You mean," Carson said as the tumult subsided, "you mean you don't really know how old you are?"

Sadie nodded. "Listen," she began, "when I was born, it was olden days, remember. Not like the kiddies today, ipsy-pipsy in a brand-new hospital—the minute they're born they got already a footprint, a fingerprint, a birth certificate and a Social Security card. When I was born, nothing was official, if you get my drift. They just knew there was another person in the house, that's all, and if you lived more than a week and a half, it was terrific."

"So you're seventy-two or seventy-five years old?"

"That's it. I mean, my father and my mother weren't exactly thrilled when I was born, to tell the truth. And what with getting out of where they were and coming to America, who could remember anything anyway? My mother always said I was born the year they had the measles epidemic, which would make me seventy-two. My father insisted it was the year Uncle Theodore went away to Kiev, which would make me three years older."

"I see," said Carson, "and when is your birthday?"

"April eighth or July thirty-first."

That little snapper, delivered with Sadie's best dead-pan expression, resulted in pandemonium. Carson rocked with laughter and rubbed tears from his eyes. It took almost a minute for a modicum of order to be restored.

"Oh, my," said Carson finally, "that is funny. But it's logical—if you're either seventy-two or seventy-five, you should have two birthdays, too."

"At least," said Sadie.

"Let's see. That makes you an Aries and a Leo."

"What are you talking?" said Sadie. "I'm Jewish!"

The audience went around the bend again. "My God," the assistant producer said to Marian, "the woman's a natural, an absolute wonder. You sure she isn't a professional actress?"

"I'm really not sure what she is," said Marian.

12

All around Marian there was chaos. Platoons of assistants and assistants-to-the-assistants were scurrying hither and yon, relaying instructions and generally getting in each other's way. Sarah Vaughan's song was the first casualty, quickly followed by the film clip showing Joe Namath in action. Mel Brooks' entrance was delayed, then delayed again until his ultimate appearance came some fifty minutes into the show. And all because of the little lady in the guest chair who was quietly bringing down the house.

For in the words of Fau Chen, a skilled pantomimist of the Manchu Court, "It is easier to push the stone downhill for ten li than to carry it upward only one." In current showbiz parlance this is roughly translated as "When you're hot, you're hot." At the moment there was no one hotter than Sadie Shapiro, and Carson shrewdly gave her her head. Between the dog food commercials and the network promos, Sadie was nothing less than a knockout. Carefully led by Carson, she told tales of her life and hard times, the words rolling off her tongue in a zany reverse English that was human, warm and endearing. Sadie was golden, Sadie was real, and best of all, completely unexpected.

Finally she was showing some samples of her work. The animal-face mittens were a smash hit, with Carson and McMahon doing a Señor Wences routine that went right over Sadie's head. And then Sadie was offering to make a sweater for Carson, getting him to stand up and remove his jacket while she measured him, and McMahon wrote down the figures. She showed him various kinds of wool and made him choose a color and a style. With all this she never got to show Carson how to knit, which was all she was expected to do in the first place.

"You are a beautiful person," Carson said as he kissed her cheek. "Please come back soon."

"Got to," said Sadie. "Making you a sweater, don't forget." With a cheery wave, she started off as the applause built; then, remembering her shopping bag, she hustled back to retrieve it, grinned sheepishly and jogged off into the wings. In thirty-two minutes, give or take a handful of commercials and station breaks, Sadie had knitted a place for herself in the fabric of American folk myth. The little old lady who had walked onstage an unknown came off a star.

A cluster of excited backstage folk surrounded Sadie as she came off, giving congratulations and shaking her hand. A crusty old stagehand leaned down to peck at her cheek. "I think I love you," he said. Sadie adored it.

"This is some old dame," the assistant producer said when the crowd had cleared. "We want her back again, while we're here in New York. Call me tomorrow and we'll set a date. And listen, I'd like you to lay off the other shows until Sadie comes back with Johnny. That should be some time next week."

"What other shows?" asked Marian.

The assistant producer laughed. "The ones who'll be calling you tomorrow morning." He looked into Marian's puzzled brown eyes. "Hey, don't tell me you don't dig what's happened here? Can't you see it? Sadie's a double-dyed wonder, an absolute natural. The kind of fresh personality who comes along once every few years and knocks people out.

"Get with it, Mrs. Wall, you've got a winner on your hands. Every talk show in America is going to want her. She can't miss. And what's more, you're going to sell about a jillion copies of her book." He turned as Sadie walked up and pumped her hand. "You are a wonderful person, Mama," he said, before trotting off to the Green Room.

Alone for the moment, Sadie and Marian regarded each other silently. "So," said Sadie finally, "that's that."

"That's that," echoed Marian.

"I went on the Johnny Carson Show and I didn't embarrass anyone."

"Right."

"I mean, maybe I was even a little good, because I heard people laughing."

"Yes," said Marian, nodding and looking at the floor, "you were probably very good." She looked up to find Sadie's eyes upon her.

"Marian, let's be honest. I was a big hit, wasn't I?"

"Sadie, you were a smash."

"That's what I thought. That's exactly what I thought." There was a weak smile on Sadie's face, and before she spoke again, she had to clear a huskiness from her throat. "A smash hit," she said quietly. "So tell me, Marian, why do you look so worried, and why don't I feel too good?"

Marian regarded the old woman for a long moment before speaking. "I think you're on the brink of something, Sadie. Fame . . . and money. And I think it may change your life. Perhaps in some ways you won't like."

Sadie nodded, her eyes downcast.

"I hope you're strong enough, Sadie."

"Like a horse. Maybe an elephant."

"And wise enough."

"Only got one head," said Sadie, unsmiling. "So what you're telling me is what I figured out for myself. It's like I'm about to cross a line. And when I do, I can never cross back again."

"Exactly, Sadie."

"All right," said Sadie, sighing, "I'm going to cross the Ruby Kahn. And what happens after that only God can say."

Stepping off the elevator in the lobby of the RCA Building, the two women found Sam Beck waiting for them. Surrounded by a cloud of blue cigar smoke, he stepped forward to greet them. "Well, well, if it isn't Helen Gurley Brown, her hairdo and her orchestra. And who is the little lady with you?"

"Hi, Sam," Sadie smiled.

"How do you like that? She talks and everything, just like a regular person. And she still remembers me. I thought, after being buddy-buddy with Johnny Carson, you wouldn't know me any more."

"Where's Bessie? Isn't she coming back with us?"

"Bessie is in the midst of reconciliation number twenty-three with Myron and Rosalie. While you two were backstage, they were kissing and crying all over each other. She's spending the night at their hotel."

"Wonderful."

"The best of both worlds," Sam said. "She still has a pair of daughters and sons-in-law to cuss out when she needs to.

"But enough of this—come here and let me kiss you, my TV star." Stepping forward, he engulfed Sadie in his arms and held her for a long moment. "Sadie, you were terrific. I got a feeling you're on your way to fame and fortune."

"She was magnificent, Mr. Beck," said Marian. "In fact, they want her back again next week."

"That's what I was afraid of," said Sam sadly. "The roar of the greasepaint, the smell of the crowd. Next week, Johnny Carson. After that, Lawrence Welk. And then poor old Sam Beck won't stand a chance."

"For Sam Beck there'll always be a chance," said Sadie, smiling. "Not a good chance, but a chance."

"At least I will escort you to a taxi, and maybe, if I'm lucky, we will even get to smooch a little on the way back to Mount Eden." He flashed Marian a look of mock-distress.

"Seventy-seven years old, and all I can get from this little woman is a kiss on the cheek. What am I, Andy Hardy?"

Outside, Marian watched as Sam helped Sadie into a cab. She saw the way he settled back, his long arm making a cradle for Sadie's head to rest on. As the taxi pulled away, he was kissing Sadie's cheek. How heartwarming it looked, and how lonely it made Marian feel.

Maybe I'll be lucky, she told herself as she began walking slowly homeward. Maybe Heathcliff will call tonight, and I'll at least have someone to talk to.

13

On the morning following Sadie's first television appearance, the telephones never stopped ringing at Harbor Press. By ten o'clock the first of what would prove to be a bushel of telegrams arrived. By eleven A.M., Marian, Jack and Arnold Hawthorne were working furiously in the publisher's office, trying to keep pace with a veritable flood of orders for Sadie's book.

"Kansas City!" Hawthorne cried triumphantly as he held a telegram aloft. "Good grief, the stores have only been open for an hour out there, and here's an order for thirty copies."

"Thirty copies," Jack Gatewood said. "In *Kansas City?*"

"Cedar Rapids, Iowa—ten copies!" Hawthorne announced.

"Another one from Chicago," Marian reported gleefully as she put the telephone down. "Who's keeping score? Jack? Fifty more copies to go to Chicago."

"Great," beamed Jack Gatewood. He consulted his master chart and made a note. "That brings us up to almost eight thousand copies in the East and six thousand in the Midwest."

"And we haven't yet heard from the West Coast," Hawthorne said.

"And she's only been on television once," Marian said.

"By God, I feel like dancing!" Hawthorne cried. Leaping to his feet, he did a wild *tour jeté,* then jigged around his desk. He shook Jack Gatewood's large hand and kissed Marian's cheek. "A winner!" he crowed, thrusting his stubby arms to heaven. "A genuine, can't-miss, best-selling winner!"

The flood of orders continued through the day and into the night as Marian, Jack and Arnold Hawthorne worked straight through without a break. Two days later, the orders were still coming in, although at a somewhat slower rate. Late in the afternoon, Hawthorne declared a moratorium on phone orders so that the staff could process all the orders already in the house, a matter of some twenty thousand copies.

"I'm worried about production," a shell-shocked Arnold Hawthorne was saying. "How are we doing in that department?"

"I've been talking to the plant all day," Jack said. "We've been guaranteed twenty-five thousand bound copies ready to be shipped by the middle of next week, with a standby order for an additional twenty-five thousand the following week."

"Not enough," said Hawthorne. "Make that fifty thousand and fifty thousand the following week."

"Impossible. They're supposed to produce three of Marian's gothics next week."

"Delay the gothics, then; I need knitting books." The publisher leaned back in his chair and ran a hand through his thinning hair. "How are the television bookings coming?" he asked Marian. "Do we have a confirmed schedule yet?"

"Not quite," she said, consulting her clipboard. "Everyone wants her, though, and the calls are still coming in."

"Give it to me roughly, then."

"Next week, of course, she goes back on The Tonight Show, as we agreed. Tentatively, Wednesday night. She's to get the star spot and they want her to do thirty minutes.

"The following morning she's on Today. I cleared it with Sadie, and she says she's going to knit ties for Frank McGee and Joe Garagiola. The following week she's on with Dick Cavett, and there's a David Frost Special she's been booked for. The next week it's Mike Douglas and Merv Griffin . . . and a Cerebral Palsy Telethon."

"A telethon?" Hawthorne said. "What's she going to do?"

"Be inspirational. She's planning to knit an American flag on camera all through the show."

"Very good. What else?"

"There are about twenty or thirty women's shows who want her. Some of them are local and some are syndicated nationwide. Your wife is coordinating those and working out a schedule."

"Never mind Mrs. Hawthorne," the publisher said. "This is too big, Marian. I want you to take charge."

Marian eyed Hawthorne for a moment and then nodded. "All right. In any case, it means we'll have to send Sadie on the road. She'll make all the local television and radio shows as she goes, and I guess we ought to coordinate luncheon club appearances and bookshop autographing parties to tie in. Which means booking hotels, laying on transportation, and getting someone to travel with Sadie as general factotum and chaperone."

"I guess you know who that's going to be," Hawthorne said. He looked at Marian's sad eyes and smiled. "Be professional, Marian. There's a job to be done—and what a job. We're at the beginning of a once-in-a-lifetime publishing dream. We've got to punch all the right buttons now, that's all. It's television that'll do the rest. Give Sadie Shapiro enough exposure on television, and there's no limit to the number of copies we can sell. But it's television that will make it happen, and from now on, Marian, that's your job."

"That figures," Jack agreed.

"I want you to personally supervise Sadie Shapiro, Marian. Stay with her. Keep her happy, keep her healthy. Hold her hand, rub her back, make her chicken soup, anything."

"She's seventy-two or seventy-five years old, Arnold," said Marian. "I hope she's strong enough to take all this."

"Nonsense! She'll outlive us all, Marian. Couldn't you see that light in her eyes on the Carson show? She was in her glory. I am positive that Sadie Shapiro is going to thrive on becoming a star."

"He's right, Marian," Jack said. "When she went jogging off into the wings, I thought she could probably run for miles."

"All right," said Marian, "let's say Sadie has enough energy. What about me? What about my life? I have a daughter at home. I just can't go charging off into the hinterlands."

"We'll hire a housekeeper for you," said Hawthorne. "Or better yet, take Laura along. It will be educational, Marian . . . and I promise there'll be no scrimping on expenses."

"I never thought I'd live to hear you say that, Arnold," Jack Gatewood said.

"Four or five weeks more in New York should handle all the nationwide media," the publisher continued, ignoring Jack. "Then you and Sadie go on the road. Say, three—maybe four months. I don't think we can sustain the book for much longer than that, but it ought to be enough."

"Oh, I almost forgot," said Jack Gatewood. "The Arts and Crafts Book Club called this morning. They want Sadie's book."

"How much do they pay?"

"Ten thousand dollars as a guarantee."

"Great!" Hawthorne said. "But I think we should resubmit Sadie to the Book-of-the-Month and the Literary Guild and let them fight it out." The publisher flashed Marian a tired smile. "I do believe we're about to get organized," he said.

~~~~~~~~~~~~~~~~~~

14

If you were one of the few people who missed seeing Sadie Shapiro's second appearance on The Tonight Show, you surely must have heard news of that rare evening by now. Many newspapers carried stories about it the following day. Sadie was the number one topic of discussion around the country. People talked about the fantastic sweater she had knitted for Johnny Carson, complete with the NBC logo and the network's peacock, resplendent on a field of bright puce, and about how Carson had stripped off his suit coat and spent the rest of the evening hosting the show in Sadie's sweater. This was not the highlight of the evening, however, and neither was Sadie's long oration concerning Doc Severinson's gold lamé coveralls. The priceless moment came when Sadie, chivvied into knitting an ensemble for Ed McMahon, attempted to take that gentleman's measurements. It was then that McMahon revealed to the world how very ticklish he was, especially under his arms, and shied away from Sadie, finally breaking into a run to escape her.

Later that evening, Sadie was booked for five more appearances on The Tonight Show. By Friday of that week, confirmed orders for twenty-five thousand copies of *Sadie Shapiro's Knitting Book* had been received by Harbor Press. At $8.95 a copy that was a lot more than chicken fat, and it meant that Sadie's royalties (less her $750 advance) came to almost $23,000. As a slightly dazed Arnold Hawthorne kept repeating to anyone who ventured within range: "And it's only the beginning."

By now the rest of the media were beginning to have a field day with Sadie. She was not just good copy, she was pure gold.

Life Magazine accompanied Sadie on her jogging trail and ran a five-page story featuring the pattern and instructions for making her sweat suit. For *Sports Illustrated,* Sadie designed a knitted Olympic Games patch that could be worked into almost any garment. *McCall's* was interested in Sadie's life-styles, former and present, and scheduled a long interview with her son, Stuart.

Sadie was featured on the women's page of *The New York Times,* along with one of her favorite recipes, and she was made the focal point of a *Sunday Times Magazine* article on the problems of the aged.

Accompanied by Marian, and sometimes by Sam Beck, Sadie appeared on five local New York radio shows (the night she spent with Long John Nebel attracted the highest rating in that show's history), and TV's Eyewitness News team had their collective eyes trained upon her.

Life was changing for Sadie Shapiro, as she had suspected it would, and it was also changing for the people around her. There was the problem of autograph seekers. In most cases, such people were stopped in Mount Eden's driveway by the small group who daily gathered there, and Sadie would be sent for to sign her name and chat for a few minutes. When Sadie was not available, however, Bessie Frankel sometimes served, pretending to be Sadie and grandly signing her friend's name.

Mail began to arrive for Sadie from all over the country, at first only a trickle, then mounting to as many as fifty letters a day. Harold Rosenbloom, with his usual good sense, collected these and sorted them for Sadie, using as his office the small neglected library. Requests for autographs were routinely handled, with Bessie Frankel pressed into service as secretary, a job she had held before the birth of her first daughter. Other letters were more difficult to answer.

"Dear Mrs. Shapiro," Harold Rosenbloom read, as Sadie knitted quietly in the armchair near the desk. "You are the only one in the world I can turn to who will understand. Last year I lost my husband after forty years of marriage. Since he's gone I can't eat or sleep or find a peaceful moment. All I can think of to do is to kill myself, I miss him so much. Please tell me what to do, Sadie."

"Ay-yi-yi," sighed Bessie, "that's a real heartache letter. That poor woman."

"Exactly," said Sadie, without missing a stitch. "So write her like this . . . 'Dear Mrs. Whatever, you should be ashamed of yourself for what you wrote me and what you're thinking. I also know the sadness of losing someone near and dear, and believe me, I loved my Reuben as much if not more than you loved your dear departed. But life doesn't go away if you just sit and stare at it. Life is, whether you like it or not, and you better like it because without it there's nothing. You must be a young woman still. Who knows what's ahead? Get yourself out, go around, see people. Give it a year, two, maybe five. To kill yourself there's always time, but never after that . . . Yours truly, Sadie Shapiro.'"

"Good, Sadie," Rosenbloom said. "Very well said. Here's another one: "'Sadie, you are my last hope; I need fifty dollars at once to buy shoes for my children. My husband ran away last month and we are broke. I know you have a good heart from seeing you on TV. Please help me . . .'"

"Fifty dollars for shoes," Sadie said, shaking her head. "It's always something with children. All right—"

"Wait," Rosenbloom interrupted, "there's more. 'P.S.: If you don't send me the money, I'm going to come to your hotel and spit right in your eye.'"

The sad look on Sadie's face changed to one of disbelief. "No, it doesn't say that."

"Read it yourself," Rosenbloom said, handing over the letter.

"Well, I'll be a cockeyed uncle . . . she *did* write that! What a nerve, to ask for money and then make a threat in the next breath. How do you answer a letter like that?"

"Like this," the tiny lawyer said. He took the letter from Sadie, crumpled it, and tossed it into the wastebasket.

"Just ignore it. Is that right, Harold?"

"In this case, yes. And in the case of about ten other letters I haven't shown you. I don't think you have to answer every letter, Sadie. Honestly, it's beginning to take up a lot of your time."

"In my book, when a person writes to you, you answer back."

"I thought you'd say that." Rosenbloom sighed and shifted the stack of letters in his hand. "I have a proposal, then. Let me handle your mail for you, with Bessie's help. The routine ones I'll take care of, the crazy ones I'll throw away, and the ones you really ought to see I'll give to you to answer."

"You'd do that for me?"

"With pleasure. What else do I have to do? Besides, it's interesting."

"It sure is," said Bessie. "I always wanted to read someone else's mail—and now I can."

"All right," said Sadie, "sold. Only promise me you won't throw away letters that ask for help, because if I can help a person even a little, I'd like to."

"Agreed," said Rosenbloom. "Although sometime soon I'd like to sit down with you and talk about money. I have some ideas."

Before Rosenbloom could go on, Sam Beck had thrust his head in the doorway. "Sadie, come quick. There's a whole women's needlepoint club outside, and Farkas is holding them in the driveway. If Adolphus sees them he'll have conniptions."

95

"Coming," said Sadie, as she put down her knitting and followed Sam down the hallway. They sneaked through the dining room, avoiding the lobby where the rotund manager might be watching, and came around the building through the back garden. At the far end of the drive they saw Abe Farkas talking to a small crowd of women, many of them holding copies of Sadie's book. As they caught sight of Sadie, they began to wave and shout, and a few broke away from Farkas and came running up the driveway.

"Head them off, Sadie, fast!" said Sam, "before they get inside and Adolphus spots them." As Sadie hesitated, Sam nudged her with his elbow. With what might have been a sigh, Sadie jogged off to intercept her fans.

Sam Beck stood where he was, watching as Sadie signed autographs. Many of the women had brought shopping bags containing their knitting, seeking advice. Naturally, Sadie could not refuse a request, and as she chatted with the women, the crowd grew. After half an hour Sam had had enough. Turning away, he walked back along the drive, trying to identify the feeling of disquiet that was growing within him each day. Sadie had become a star now, and clearly, her life was no longer her own. The trouble was, there was less of her life to be shared with someone named Samuel Joseph Beck.

15

Juan Otero's taxi was waiting as Marian came dashing out of the Grindl Building in mild disarray. "We going to Mount Eden?" Juan asked. Marian nodded. *"Bueno,* I have a good shortcut by now."

Once in Queens, Juan cut off the expressway and drove through quiet, tree-lined streets. "That is some *pistolera,* that Sadie," he called back to Marian. "When she chases the big McMahon the other night, I thought my Carmelita would fall off the bed . . . She going to do another TV show soon?"

"Yes. Later today . . . a David Frost Special. Oh, God!" Marian suddenly cried. "I just remembered something. Wide World of Sports is taping Sadie jogging this afternoon . . . and I forgot to tell Sadie! Hurry, Juan."

Juan's cab rounded the corner of Hollis Avenue and came rolling up to Mount Eden. Parked along the drive was a station wagon marked "ABC News," and blocking the drive was a small mob of men and women who came running toward Marian as she got out of the taxi. A woman with plastic rollers in her hair thrust a notebook under Marian's nose. "Sign my book!" she shrieked in a voice that cut to the bone. Behind her, two more women crowded forward, pushing Marian against the cab. Another woman, even more aggressive, reached out and slapped a ballpoint pen into Marian's hand. "Are you anybody?" she demanded.

"Please, please," Marian pleaded shrilly, as the mob forced her back against the cab.

"She's nobody," the plastic-haired lady said, and

as quickly as they had come, the group was gone up the drive, congregating again at the ABC wagon.

Somewhat shaken, Marian walked slowly to the lobby entrance only to find her way barred by the ancient elevator operator. "Go away," he said, his arms folded across his chest. "Nobody gets in without they have a pass."

"It's me, Sadie Shapiro's editor. Remember?"

"Oh, yes," the old man said, his eyes focusing, "the Commonist troublemaker herself. You I got orders to let in. Report to the manager's office across the lobby."

Marian found Sam Beck sitting with the manager. "Here's Sadie's editor," Beck said. "Tell her what you told me."

"How do you do, Mrs. Wall," the manager said politely.

"Don't let him fool you with his manners, Marian," said Sam. "He's a slippery article."

Adolphus grinned nervously and cocked his head. "Mr. Beck is just one of the crosses I bear, Mrs. Wall. As if there weren't enough problems here today."

"Problems," Sam snorted. "Somebody says he doesn't like tapioca pudding, and with Adolphus that becomes a *problem.*"

"Oh, I think we have more than tapioca on our hands this time," the manager said in a self-satisfied way. "There are rules here at Mount Eden, and they are meant to be followed."

"Rules," echoed Sam Beck. "I know what you'd like, Adolphus—for everyone to take three tranquilizers a day and walk around in carpet slippers like a bunch of zombies. That's what you'd really like, isn't it?"

"I shall choose to ignore that," the manager said. He glared at Beck for an instant and turned his small eyes on Marian. "Mrs. Wall, I insist that Mrs. Shapiro end this disturbance at once. Mount Eden is a hotel for senior citizens, many of them infirm, and all of them demanding a certain level of dignity and decorum. I cannot permit their rights to privacy and order to be overridden by this—this—*public relations circus!*"

"I'm terribly sorry if you've been inconvenienced, Mr. Adolphus. I had no idea that things had gotten so out of hand."

"The last days of Pompeii," the manager interrupted. "What Mrs. Shapiro has created at Mount Eden is nothing short of outrageous. Cameras and flashbulbs everywhere you turn. People tramping through our petunia beds. Do you know that a group of fans sneaked in here for dinner last night, and some of them stole silverware? And that a man from some underground newspaper tried to follow Mildred Futterman into the women's sauna this morning?"

"Really? Well," Marian said lamely, "the tree of fame sometimes bears bitter fruit. Perhaps if Sadie hadn't given Mount Eden's address on The Tonight Show, things wouldn't be so bad. I'll try to make some other arrangements for her next interviews."

"That's not good enough," Adolphus said flatly. "There are to be no further interviews at Mount Eden, Mrs. Wall. None. And furthermore, I demand that you get rid of that crowd of curiosity-seekers who have descended upon us. At once."

"How's that for rotten, Marian?" Sam Beck said. "Isn't he a prize?"

"You mean those people in the street?" asked Marian. "Surely you must see that we have no control over them. How could we possibly influence them?"

A slow smile played over Adolphus' lips as his fat fingers drummed busily on the desk top. "There is a way," he smirked. "Very simple."

"You mean you want Sadie to leave? Is that it?"

"You said leave, Mrs. Wall, I didn't. And now that you mention it, I think it's a perfectly wonderful idea. Say—this afternoon sometime, before six." Icicles dripped from his smile.

"Now I know where Martin Bormann went," Sam Beck observed. He held out his cigar and deliberately flicked an inch of ash to the carpeted floor.

"Now see here, Mr. Adolphus," said Marian, "that's unfair, and I'm not going to let you get away with it."

"That's where you're wrong," the manager purred, pointing a stubby finger. "I am perfectly within my rights. Mrs. Shapiro signed a rental agreement when she came to Mount Eden. That agreement gives me the power to dispossess her at my discretion. As far as I'm concerned, she has violated five or six different rules of behavior. Did I say violated? She's gone and kicked hell out of them." He began to tick off points on his fingers. "Conducting business affairs from this address. Violent or unruly visitations. Entertaining parties of more than five visitors without permission. Causing, or having others cause on her behalf, damage to property. Disrespect for the normal rights of other tenants . . ."

"Where are you, King Kong, now that we need you?" groaned Sam Beck.

"Six o'clock, Mrs. Wall," Adolphus said stiffly. "If she leaves by then, I won't have her thrown out. And by God, she's lucky I don't sue her for the madhouse she's turned this place into. That's it. As far as I'm concerned, this meeting is over." With that, the manager came out from behind the desk, waddled swiftly across the room and left, slamming the door closed behind him.

For a brief moment, Marian and Sam Beck exchanged glances, consternation showing in Marian's troubled eyes. "What a mess," she said.

The corners of Sam's mouth turned up and he came as close to smiling as he ever did. "I don't know about that," he observed, looking at the end of his cigar. "It could be the biggest break I ever had."

100

16

"Here she comes now," said Howard Cosell into the microphone as the television crew snapped into action. "That woman you see jogging toward our ABC camera . . . that seventy-two-or-seventy-five-year-old woman who has captured the hearts and minds of the nation . . . a testament to the fact that you are only as old as you feel—Sadie Shapiro, ladies and gentlemen, grandmother, jogger, world-class knitting champion . . ."

The TV director's instructions came through the intercom button tucked into Cosell's ear. "Call her to the microphone, Howard . . . ready . . . *now!*"

"Mrs. Shapiro? Sadie Shapiro . . . this is Howard Cosell . . ."

"Where's she going?" the voice in Cosell's ear shouted. "She's not stopping . . . she missed her cue!"

"And there she goes," said Cosell without missing a beat, "jogging her way back to the now-famous Mount Eden Senior Citizens Hotel . . . Sadie Shapiro . . . inspiration to the world . . . her short, choppy strides a textbook picture of perfect jogging form . . ."

Train, don't strain, Sadie told herself as she bounced along to the corner of the street and turned toward home. The next two hundred yards would complete the mile and one-half course, and she felt fine. Ahead of her, down the street, people lined the curb. Crazy. Coming out to see an old woman in a sweat suit. Didn't they have anything better to do? And the camera crew on top of the station wagon. A mob scene ahead, any way you looked at it.

Sadie skipped onto the sidewalk, then darted, quick as a shadow, down the alley that would bring her through Mount Eden's service entrance and into the back garden.

"The athlete is back," Mrs. Bradie called out to no one in particular as Sadie paused and slowed to a walk. "What's the matter, big shot, you're not in the mood for autographs today?"

Sadie walked by, her proud head erect. Bradie had turned sour, like many of the others. That much was clear. When she had first come to Mount Eden, they had ignored her. Because they knew even then that she was different and that different wasn't always a good thing. And then, the book. They'd liked that, and they'd helped her enormously. But now? She had become *too* famous, that was the story. Much too famous for their liking. People in a group did strange things, Sadie thought, because in a group one or two can think for all, and that's never a good idea. People. How could you figure them out?

From the doorway that led into the back garden, Marian and Sam Beck stood watching Sadie appear. "Look at her, Marian," Sam sighed. "Is that a fine figure of a woman or not? You know, the first time I saw her she was jogging. I knew right then she was something different. Because when she came jogging by in that tight sweat suit, nothing jiggled. That's my Sadie."

"Your Sadie is a woman without a home at the moment, Sam. Who's going to give her the bad news?"

"Oh, me, of course. Because there's something I got to say anyway that may make it easier."

But before Sam could speak, Sadie did. "Marian, Sam . . . I just decided something. I'm leaving Mount Eden. Any place that doesn't want me, then I don't want. So I'm getting out of here, the faster the sooner."

"Funny you should mention that," said Sam.

"But first I'm going upstairs to take a shower. Then later we have a date with David Frost, right, Marian?"

Sam took Sadie's elbow and held it. "First, take a little walk with me in the garden, Sadie. I got something important to say, and I don't think it can wait."

Sadie's eyebrows arched as she shot a quizzical look at Marian, but she allowed herself to be led away down the garden path.

"Beautiful day, isn't it?" Sam said, as he fumbled for a way to begin.

"That's what you got on your mind, Beck, a weather report?"

"Sadie, give a fella a chance. Let me get started."

"Wouldn't say another word . . ."

Sam held his cigar at arm's length and contemplated the tip of it. "Look, what you just said, about leaving Mount Eden. That's been on my mind for some time, Sadie. And one thing I got to say—if you go, I go—I made up my mind on that score a long time ago."

"Congratulations. So there'll be two less for dinner."

"Sadie," Sam said, squeezing her elbow. "Look," he began again, "what I mean is this. Until you moved into Mount Eden, I thought everything was over with me. Seventy-seven years old, Sadie, and I figured it was wrapped up. Life was boring. There was nothing to do. I was going out of my mind and waiting for the end. You know what I did all day before you got here? To amuse myself, I'd shave. That's right. I'd start in the morning after breakfast and lather up my face for maybe half an hour, and then I'd very, very slowly shave my chin. That's all, just my chin.

"Then I'd wait a while and lather up again and maybe do one cheek. Or maybe my upper lip.

"And I'd wash off and go smoke a cigar, and then come back and do my other cheek. And in that way I could pass a whole morning. I'm telling you, I couldn't wait for my beard to grow back so I could start over again."

"Beck, you're a little crazy, you know that?"

"Not a little, a lot. Crazy for you, Sadie. Because the minute you got on the scene, so to speak, my whole life changed. Peppy, Sadie, I had forgotten about peppy. That's the way I used to be until my wife, let her rest, passed away. And you showed me that if you let yourself go you can turn into a vegetable. Compared to you, don't you see, that's what I was. A turnip. Maybe a rutabaga.

"But you were my example, and I woke myself up. However much time I got left, let me live it like a person—that's what you showed me, Sadie. And from that minute until now, I stayed as close to you as I am now. Not that I would mind getting a little closer," he added, slipping his arm around her waist.

"Control yourself, Beck," said Sadie.

"And now you're going to move away, and that's why I'm talking. Because I can't let you go without I tell you what's laying here inside on my heart. I need you, Sadie. I want you. I don't want a day to pass by without us being together."

"Beck, don't squeeze," Sadie said as she removed his arm from her waist.

"I need you, I want you, I probably even love you, Sadie. So let's move out of here, today. We'll go to a hotel. And then we'll find a little apartment, and that'll be it. Sadie Shapiro and Sam Beck, together at last, now and forever."

At this last, Sadie stopped walking and turned to face Sam. Her face was impassive, but behind her eyes a tiny fire glowed. "So that's it, Beck? Your big proposition? I should move in with you, right?"

"That's the story, Sadie, to live happily ever after."

"You're going to marry me, Beck?"

Beck coughed and a puff of blue smoke flew out of his

mouth to hover over his head. *"Who* married? *What* married? Did I say anything about marrying?"

The corners of Sadie's mouth curled down and she shook her head. "A proposition like yours I could hear on the street. I don't need it from an old friend."

"Sadie, please, marriage for people our age is out of the question. Who's going to say anything if we live together? My God, I'm seventy-seven and you're—how old you are. We each have a little money. And with our Social Security, we can have a life."

"Hah!" said Sadie. "It always comes down to that with you, Beck. Always you're after moofki-poofki."

"As God is my witness, Sadie, that's the furthest thing from my mind. Moofki-poofki? Phooey!"

"Sure, sure."

"All right, a little moofki-poofki. It's only natural, I'm not a Stonewall Jackson. You know about my prostate. Believe me, the organ at the Paramount Theater was probably in better condition than—"

"Hold it! Don't talk dirty."

"Come live with me and be my companion. Sadie . . . please."

Hands clasped behind her back, Sadie walked a few steps away and then paced back. "Not until the ring is on the finger, Sam Beck," she declared. "A Shapiro doesn't move in with a person until there's a meeting of the minds and a meeting with a rabbi."

"Marriage is out of the question, Sadie. I mean it's ridiculous. A woman, seventy-two or seventy-five years old . . ."

"Who never slept in the same bed with a man who wasn't her husband. And at my age, I'm certainly not going to start now. So if there's a decent proposal somewhere on your lips, Sam Beck, I'm getting all ready to hear it."

"I swore on my wife's deathbed I would never marry again. It wouldn't be right. I can't marry you, Sadie. Please

105

don't ask that. But I know you care for me, and by God, I'd do anything for you."

"Except marry me."

"Come, Sadie, let's find an apartment. You'll teach me how to jog and knit, and I'll show you how to play klabejass. Sadie, please."

"Sam Beck, you're a fine man, and I probably love you a little in the bargain. But until I hear from you a few words that begin, 'Will you marry me?'—I'm not going to be listening. So goodbye, Sam Beck." Tears flooded Sadie's eyes as she watched Beck's face fall. Without thinking, she stepped forward and held him close, then kissed him squarely and passionately on his lips. "So goodbye, Sam Beck," she repeated and walked away.

17

As Juan's cab pulled away from the Mount Eden doorstep, Sadie kept looking back through the rear window, seeing the ruined petunia bed, the grassy lawn, the few people who had stood by to say a quiet goodbye. Of these last there were not many, and Sam Beck was not one of them. And that hurt most of all.

"You never know what's around the corner in this life, do you?" Sadie said as Mount Eden faded from view. "So now it's goodbye, Mount Eden—hello, Manhattan, and who can tell what's going to happen tomorrow."

"Something wonderful, no doubt," said Marian, making an effort to be cheerful. For in all the time she had known Sadie she had never seen her as distraught as she appeared now. The sparkle was gone, that inner glow that made Sadie the special person she was. Rather too quickly, Marian turned the conversation to the latest sales figures of the book. Fifty thousand copies were now in print, and the book was selling at the rate of ten thousand copies a week. If that continued, she informed Sadie, there was a good chance that the book would make *The New York Times* list of best sellers. And that listing, if it happened, would spur the sale of even more copies.

None of this news seemed to cheer Sadie's mood.

"At my age, to have trouble with a man," Sadie said. She looked out at the crowded expressway and slowly shook her head.

"I don't think age counts in those matters," Marian observed. "It seems to me that it must go on forever."

Sadie turned and looked closely at Marian. "Marian, would you sleep with a man who wasn't your husband?"

Marian slowly smiled, thinking of the colonel who had never returned and of the absence of men in her life thereafter. "I'm no expert, Sadie, not when it comes to love. And from where I sit, I can't give anyone advice on men."

Sadie sighed and shifted in her seat. "I'm going to miss him, Sam Beck. And I'm thinking, maybe, Sadie, you made a mistake. A man like Sam is no Tom, Dick or Harry. He's got a lot of fine qualities. Still, when you're brought up one way and you live your whole life according to certain rules, it's very hard to change. What Sam wants I couldn't do in a million years. And especially not tomorrow." Brightening, Sadie put a smile on her face. She reached over and clasped Marian's hand. "I'm lucky I've got you, Marian. You're a good friend to have. Are you sure you have room to put me up for a while? Until I find another place to live?"

"I'm positive," Marian said. She squeezed Sadie's hand. "And I'm happy to have you. With all the interviews we have coming up in the next few weeks, it'll make sense for us to be together. And I'm sure you'll be comfortable in my study."

"I don't want to interfere with your life, Marian. That wouldn't be fair. After all, you've done so much for me already. I wouldn't be where I am today if it wasn't for you."

Sadie's eyes met Marian's as her last words echoed between them. Marian smiled and then giggled, and then Sadie was laughing, and then they were both laughing.

"Oh, Marian, when I went on that show with Johnny Carson, who knew that life would never be the same? Who knew that we would be opening a Van Doren box? That people would be running after me for autographs? Autographs, from me, a woman who never got past the eighth grade! I'm telling you, this is some crazy America we're living in."

"It's winner take all, Sadie, and right now you're a winner."

"Hoo-ha! Some winner. Meanwhile, tell me about your Laura. What's she like?"

Marian chuckled ruefully and smiled. "I wish I really knew, Sadie. What is Laura like? She's twelve and living with me, but I can't really say we get along well, or that I understand her. There's a coolness between us. I think she has just lately realized that most families come equipped with a father, and she resents not having one quite terribly."

"If a marriage doesn't work out it's between a man and a woman. It's not for children to say."

"Of course, Sadie. But still . . . there it is. And I think, because of this feeling, Laura wants to punish me. So she purposely does things that will make me angry, and we argue, and make up, and argue some more. She has a weight problem, too, and I suspect it stems from this underlying frustration."

"Trouble with a child is like a stone in your heart. Sad, very sad. And how big are her feet?"

"Her what?"

"Her feet. I thought, on the way to the studio, I would knit her a pair of slippers. Pass me my knitting bag, won't you, and then tell me all about that David Frost person I'm going to meet."

Some hours later, it was probable that David Frost would soon be telling people about that Sadie Shapiro he had met. For Sadie's appearance on his Special had thrown the studio audience, and the affable young Englishman too, into a fit of laughter. Most of his British circumlocutions were lost on Sadie, and when he tried to explain his meaning, he found he could not easily follow Sadie's words. In the resulting confusion, only one question and answer stood out. It came when Frost, as is his custom, asked Sadie for her own definition of love.

"Love," Sadie said, "love means never having to say you're sorry, but you say it anyway . . . because, after all, if you love someone you want to make sure you don't hurt their feelings . . . so you say it anyway, whether you mean it or not, because a human being is a human being, and we each have our own ways and feelings, and if in the end you don't have respect for each other, then what do you have?"

"I don't know," asked a puzzled Frost, "what does one have?"

"Me, you're asking?" shrugged Sadie.

Frost stared at her, and for the first time in eons uncrossed his legs. He also invited Sadie back for another appearance on his show.

Outside the studio, as Sadie and Marian walked to Juan's cab, Sam Beck stepped in front of them. "Well, well, if it isn't the star herself and her friend, Clare Boothe Luce."

Sadie's heart leaped up at the sight of him, but she held herself in check. "Sam, what are you doing here?"

"Oh, I don't know," he said coolly, eyebrows raised, "just passing by. I brought a few things you left behind I thought you might need. And the rest of your clothing I packed myself. If you'll tell me where you're going to be staying, I'll see that they're delivered."

"That's very nice of you, Sam. I'll be with Marian for a while."

"Uh-huh," said Sam, "I see. By the way, starting tomorrow I'll be looking for an apartment myself. I wondered if there was any neighborhood you preferred."

"Oh, I see," said Sadie, adopting Beck's cool tone of voice. "Yes, there is a neighborhood I like. Near City Hall, where the marriage licenses are."

"Is that so?" Sam deadpanned. "I've been in that neighborhood myself, and I don't plan on going back."

"That's up to you."

"Aha. As long as I'm asking, do you prefer one bedroom or two?"

"That depends on whether the man is my husband or not," said Sadie.

"Put down the hammer," said Beck. "I got the message." He took a long pull on his cigar and looked despairingly at Marian. "Would you believe a woman seventy-two or seventy-five years old is worrying about her virtue? Is that ridiculous, Marian?"

"Don't talk to Marian," Sadie cut in. "This is between you and me, Beck. Now if you'll excuse me, I've got to run. I don't like to stand on street corners talking to strange old men."

"Permit me," said Beck, swooping into a low bow. He opened the taxi door and helped the women step inside. Closing the door, he bent down to look in at the open window. "Take care of yourself, Sadie," he said. "Marian, make sure she eats and gets her rest."

"Goodbye, Sam," Sadie said.

"Not goodbye," said Sam Beck, a thin smile on his lips. "I don't quit so easy. I'll be around, Sadie, just waiting until you come to your senses."

"You might be waiting a long time," Sadie said.

"We'll see. In the meantime, remember—Sam Beck has just begun to fight."

~~~~~~~~~~~~~~~~

18

It was after nine o'clock in the evening of what had been a long and trying day. Comfortable in body if not in mind, Sadie sat at the dinette table. Her fingers, as always, were operating in top gear, reaching down now and then to free a loop of green wool from the basket at her feet. In another few hours of work, Virginia Graham would have a pants suit à la Shapiro. Across the table, behind a mountainous pile of paper, Marian sat reading a manuscript. From time to time she would engage the pencil in her poised left hand and scribble furiously. A pair of tortoise shell "work" eyeglasses perched on her nose kept sliding tableward as she read, and her hand would flash up to hold them in a graceful, unconscious gesture.

Laura, not yet in bed, was in her room playing records on her stereo set, punctuating the quiet scene in the dinette. "It's all right to pollute my body, baby," some slurred male voice shrieked, "but don't you go pollutin' my mind . . ."

Sadie and Marian exchanged a glance, Marian wincing as the second chorus came around and was introduced by shrilly acid guitars. "Is that too loud, Sadie?"

"What?" asked Sadie. "I couldn't hear you, the music's so loud."

Sighing, Marian walked heavily to Laura's room and closed the door behind her. Sadie heard a few shouted words go back and forth between mother and daughter, and then Marian returned. The stereo was silent.

Obviously upset, Marian went back to her reading. Laura

was apparently everything that Marian had said she was, and perhaps a little more. Her greeting upon Marian's arrival with Sadie this evening had been very cool. In fact, Sadie could recall several landlords who had been more gracious. Twelve years old, she thought, was a difficult age.

Marian put down her pencil, took off her glasses, and closed the top manuscript on the pile. She ran a hand across her eyes. "Would you like a cup of tea, Sadie?"

"No, thanks. In fact, I was only staying up to keep you company while you were working."

"Don't wait for me," Marian said, stretching. "I'm going to be at this for hours."

"Really?" said Sadie, surprise showing on her face. "Must be important, then, right?"

Marian shrugged. "It's work. Two more gothics. I swear, sometimes I can't tell where one ends and the next one begins."

"I gather you don't like them too much."

"It's a job, like any other. And it doesn't hurt anyone, I guess. Actually, the one I'm working on now isn't too bad."

"And what are you doing to it?"

"Editing it."

"Aha! Editing. At last I'll find out what that is."

Marian laughed. "It's not that easy to explain, Sadie. Sometimes I do little more than read a manuscript and say, 'very good.' That is a rare occasion, though. Mostly it involves cutting a story down to size." She gathered the heavy manuscript and held it up for Sadie to see. "Right now, I'm trying to change this nine-hundred-page marshmallow of a story into a five-hundred-page lean greyhound. I'm chopping out scenes, characters, subplots that go on and on until they put the reader to sleep."

Sadie nodded, her lips pursed. "Sounds like a terrifically hard job, Marian."

"Sometimes. But it's often very exciting. Take our biggest

113

gothic of the past few years, *Hardcastle Castle*. When I got that manuscript it was actually a contemporary romance set in Yugoslavia, about a woodcutter and a young girl. The last four hundred pages, as I recall, were a strong plea for Serbo-Croatian unity."

"But who would read that?"

"Exactly. So I suggested that the locale be changed to nineteenth-century England, that the hero be a local baron who owned a useless coal mine, and the love interest become a young governess whose father had just patented a new sort of miner's lamp. It worked like a charm."

"No kidding, Marian? Boy, they must pay you a lot of money for what you do and how hard you work."

"They pay me what they pay me, Sadie. Arnold Hawthorne isn't widely known as a big spender." Marian got up and went into the kitchen to get her cigarettes. She came back, found an ashtray, and seated herself nearer Sadie. "Maybe some of it is my fault," she said, after a moment. "You know, Harbor Press is the only place I've ever worked in publishing. In many ways, I suppose, Arnold looks on me as a switchboard operator who made good."

"Hey, Marian, that's no reason not to pay you what you're worth. After all, a girl who sticks in one place shows loyalty, right?"

Marian's laugh had a bitter edge to it. "It doesn't work that way, Sadie. Unfortunately. I've seen others get promoted ahead of me who, frankly, didn't deserve it."

"I knew I didn't like that Arnold Hawthorne the minute I saw him. So why don't you go work somewhere else?"

"Why?" She looked away across the room, her mouth a tight line.

Sadie reached out and took Marian's hand. "I'm getting too personal. Excuse me."

"No," said Marian, "perhaps it's good. You know, I've

gone along for years now without questioning things. Life falls into a pattern."

"Don't tell me about patterns. That I know about. You wake up one day and everything's behind you. The design is finished, and you don't like it. Don't be that way, Marian, I mean it. You're terrific at what you do. So if you don't get respect at Harbor Press, go someplace else. A girl with your brains, your looks . . ."

"Let's not get into my looks," Marian said. "I'm not too smashing in that department to judge by the results."

"I've been meaning to talk to you about your hair," Sadie said.

"You wouldn't be the first one."

"But that can wait. First, I'm going to call Arnold Hawthorne tomorrow and tell him a thing or two."

"Sadie, don't," Marian said sharply. "Hawthorne is my problem, not yours. And Laura is my problem."

"Laura's problem is fifteen pounds. That's all. She'd be a different child if she lost some weight."

"Maybe. And maybe it's me."

Sadie looked closely at Marian and sighed. "You are what you are, Marian. If you don't like it, then change what you are. A girl with your brains and beauty—you could be anything you want. You should get a raise, and a promotion and a haircut. And men should come flocking to your door."

"The only man in my life is a voice on the telephone," said Marian. "And the only reason I talk to him at all is because I'm so lonely." Tears brimmed in Marian's eyes, and she began to weep softly.

Sadie reached over and held a warm hand on her shoulder. "Ay-yi-yi," she said, "forgive me."

"Oh, Sadie," Marian sobbed, smiling through her tears, "I feel better than I have in a long, long time."

"How much longer is she going to be around?" Laura Wall asked between bites. With a heavy hand, she spooned a large mound of marmalade onto a scrap of toast and crammed it into her mouth.

Marian took a bitter sip of her morning coffee and regarded her daughter with a baleful eye. "Chew, darling, don't just swallow," she said. A look of anger crossed Laura's face, but Marian ignored it and stared the girl down. "Mrs. Shapiro is our guest," she went on, "and she's only been here a few days."

Laura mumbled something between bites which could only be malicious. Marian decided to let it pass. "In just a few weeks, we'll be starting our cross-country trip—you and Sadie and me—and we'll have lots of fun, Laura, I promise." A smug smile turned the corners of Laura's mouth skyward. Marian's throat tightened. Whenever she held out her hand in friendship to Laura, it usually got bitten. All right, she told herself, starting very soon, I become strict. And the first order of business would be a diet.

Lighting a cigarette, Marian watched Laura eat. And eat. Somewhere beneath those round cheeks, there had to be bones, it was an anatomical certainty. And someday—dear God, when?—the girl might even have a waistline.

"Good morning, everyone," came a warm voice. If Sadie had heard Laura's last words, her face did not show it. Looking fresh and wearing a starched bright floral housecoat, she was the essence of cheerfulness.

"Can I make you some breakfast, Sadie?" Marian asked.

"No, thanks. I already know where the saltines are, and my cottage cheese I picked up the other day. I'll put up some water for my tea. If I have my cottage cheese, saltines and tea, I have breakfast." She drew some water and put it on the stove to boil, then seated herself at the table next to Laura. "So don't say good morning, sleepyhead, see if I care," she said, winking.

"Good morning," Laura said briefly. She took a large bite of her cupcake and stared out the window.

"A cupcake with chocolate icing," Sadie mused. "All sugar and no protein. Every cupcake puts about half a pound of weight on you."

If Laura heard, she didn't answer. She reached out to the box on the table and put another cupcake on her plate. Marian's eyes flashed a protective warning to Sadie, but it went unheeded.

"There's protein, you see," Sadie went on, "and there's what I call *anti*-teen. Protein is what makes your body run—after all, the body is a machine—and anti-teen is what runs you down. Believe me, a cupcake is right on top of the list of anti-teens. Only thing worse is maybe a Mallomar."

"We're fresh out of those," said Marian breezily. "Laura likes a big breakfast. It's one of her favorite meals. In fact, come to think of it, every meal is one of her favorite meals."

"So I see," said Sadie, as Laura kept chewing steadily. "Believe me, if everybody ate more cottage cheese, there wouldn't be such trouble in the world today. Cottage cheese is right up there on top of my list of protein. Along with boiled liver, which is the best, but nobody can eat it."

"Boiled liver?" Laura said. "Yuch!"

"Laura hates liver," said Marian.

"Can't blame her. How about chopped liver?"

"I don't think she's ever had it. Have you, Laura?"

117

"Chopped liver, yuch!" said Laura, between bites of her second cupcake.

"So what do you like?" Sadie asked.

The young girl cleared her mouth with a swig of chocolate milk. "Pizza, mostly."

"With the oil and the tomato sauce and a million spices?"

"And frankfurters."

"Eat a frankfurter and you take your life in your mouth."

"Tuna fish sandwiches on toast."

"That's all right—plenty of protein."

"But only with a ton of mayonnaise."

"Of course."

"Peanut butter and jelly sandwiches."

"About a million calories."

"Washed down by a Coke."

"That's to complete the damage, I suppose," said Sadie, shaking her head. "That's quite a little list."

Laser beams shot out of Laura's eyes and pinned Sadie to the wall. Marian jumped into the breach and reminded Laura of the time, telling her not to be late for school. With dark looks and much loud slamming of doors and drawers, Laura collected her schoolbooks and came back to stand in the kitchen doorway. "Is Mrs. Shapiro going to be here when I come home from school?" she asked, her chin upraised in Mussolini fashion.

"Yes," said Marian, looking her daughter straight in the eye.

The girl left the apartment without another word.

For a few moments there was only the sound of a pot of water coming to a boil on the stove. Sadie rose and went about the business of making a cup of tea. Marian sipped her coffee and stared at the wall. "Now you know everything," she said.

"Well, maybe I shouldn't have started up with her," Sadie said, sitting down with her tea.

"Don't blame yourself. Laura and I have arguments every day, it seems, whether anyone's here or not."

Sadie took a sip of hot tea. "I think Laura doesn't like herself too much," she said, "so maybe it's hard for her to like anyone else. You know, sometimes developing a shape like a pear can also give you a chip on your shoulder."

"Could be," Marian agreed, "but diet days are coming. I've made up my mind about that."

"Good."

"And I've been thinking about our talk of the other night. I'm going to beard Arnold Hawthorne in his den. I'm tired of being underpaid and overlooked."

"Congratulations. I'm behind you a hundred percent."

"Yipes!" said Marian, glancing at the clock, "I'm late. I'm going to hop into the shower and then scoot. If the office should call, tell them I'm on my way."

Sadie watched Marian hastily leave the kitchen; a few moments later she heard the low thrum of the shower begin. She sipped her tea and nibbled a few bites of cottage cheese. Maybe there was a way to help Marian with Laura's weight problem? But how? She couldn't interfere too much between mother and daughter. And yet, since she was living here for a while, she might lend a hand. Bribery? Was that the answer? What was it that would motivate the girl?

The sound of the telephone interrupted Sadie's thoughts. She went to the living room and picked up the phone on the second ring.

"Cortina d'Ampezzo at twilight," said Heathcliff, "with the snow falling gently on your hair. The two of us at the top of the ski lift . . . you smiling as . . ."

It must be my bad ear, Sadie thought, because I can't be hearing what I'm hearing. She shifted the receiver.

". . . grasping you to me, I whisper in your ear . . ."

"Whoa! Whoa!" said Sadie, "say no more. Who is this?"

There was a sharp intake of breath on the other end. "I'm awfully sorry," Sadie heard the voice say. "Excuse me."

Still shaking her head, Sadie put the phone down as Marian, her head wrapped in a towel, peeked out of the bathroom door. "Was that for me, Sadie?"

Sadie stared at Marian, then smiled. "Marian, if that was for you, we're both in a lot of trouble."

~~~~~~~~~~~~~~~~

20

After Marian had left for the office, Sadie wandered about the small apartment. She felt lonely and deserted, and for the first time in many years, she felt old. Too restless to knit, she had time to reflect on every ache and pain, and of these there were many. Come on now, she told herself, you know what to do. Keep your head and your hands busy, and your body will take care of itself. So saying, she showered and dressed. Then, like a pint-sized dynamo, she whirled about the house making beds, straightening books and ashtrays, dusting the furniture. Then she took up her knitting bag and plunged in. In rapid order she polished off a cap and scarf for Laura.

Laura . . . the problem hung on in her head. What to do? When the telephone rang, she approached it gingerly.

"Sadie," said Sam Beck, "I'm going out of my mind. I'm so bored I think I'm going to kill myself just to break the monotony."

"Take a cold bath or a hot shower. Sam, how are you?"

"How am I, she asks? Seventy-seven and feeling every minute of it. Yesterday, do you know what I did? I went to Staten Island to buy a newspaper. That's right. A bus to the train, the train to the ferry, bought a paper and went back to Mount Eden. Is that a way to kill four hours? Is this a life? Sadie, please, let's get together."

"Sam . . ."

"Listen, Sadie . . . a stranger said 'hello' to me yesterday, I almost kissed him. Sadie, please, I have to be where you are and do what you do and go where you go, and I'll be happy."

"Sam, no song and dance. I gave you my last and final word, and you know what to do."

"Marriage is out of the question. Sadie, I'm not a rich man, but a little money I got. And a lot of insurance. But Sadie, I also got two kids and four grandchildren, and believe me, they've spent all that money already. It wouldn't be right to get married."

"What is this with money? Did I ever mention that word in your presence?"

"Sadie, please . . ."

"I'm talking principle, Beck. You know what I'm after. A little gold ring in a little blue box."

"All right," said Sam Beck, "you want to get into a stubborn contest, I'll play your game. I'll show you I can be just as pigheaded as you are. We'll just go on making each other miserable until you give up."

"Never," said Sadie.

"We'll see," said Sam Beck.

There was a long silence while both parties listened to each other's heavy breathing. Then Beck said, in a low voice: "Sadie . . . I love you."

"Sam, I love you."

"Sadie, I'm going to miss you."

"I miss you already, Sam."

Tears filled Sadie's eyes as she put down the telephone. But by an effort of will she held them back, then dashed to the bathroom and scrubbed her face in cold water. In the mirror she looked at herself. Author, she said to herself mockingly, famous person! So what are you trying to do? Principles come first, her other self answered. Seventy-two or seventy-five years of morality you don't change overnight. You've got to stick up for what's right—even if it kills you.

Not feeling much better, she wandered through the apartment. Maybe if she thought about Laura, she wouldn't think about Sam. She walked into the girl's room and sat on a chair near her desk. Make believe you are Laura Wall, she thought. Okay. Now what would be on your mind today? What would make you start behaving yourself—would even make you go on a diet?

On the wall above Laura's bed, faces stared down at Sadie. Posters hung with cellophane tape. David Cassidy smiling, David Cassidy jumping, David Cassidy playing a guitar. Bobby Sherman on a bicycle, Bobby Sherman singing, Bobby Sherman eating a popsicle. Beyond these there were dozens of other young faces cut from magazines and plastered to the wall.

Of course. It was obvious. When Laura wasn't thinking about food, she thought about the faces on the wall. Boys. With long hair, white smiles, and guitars. Singers, musicians. The people who played that music she was all the time listening to. Right. The minute she woke up in the morning the radio went on. And when she came home from school, same thing. The radio and her records.

No doubt about it, thought Sadie, what keeps a girl in shape is a boy. An idea began to form. Thinking about it, she walked to the phone in the living room and dialed Bessie's son-in-law, Myron.

"Hello, Sadie the famous TV personality and author," said Myron. "And how are you today?"

"Needing a favor, Myron."

"For you, anything. Shoot."

"Myron, do you have on your program any of these what-do-you-call-'em—rock-and-roll singers?"

"You call them Rock artists, and we have them, sure. What's up?"

"Is anyone on tonight? I mean, in town right now?"

"Let me see. Yeah. Tonight we have Ronnie Porter and Canned Fruit."

"Canned Fruit? This is the name of a person?"

"No," said Myron, laughing. "It's a group. Mostly it's a singer named Ronnie Porter and two other guys who back him up."

"Ronnie Porter? Canned Fruit? Listen, would they appeal maybe to a twelve-year-old girl? Would she know them . . . or him?"

"Haven't you heard 'I Wanna Eat Your Nose?' It's right up there on the charts. Every twelve-year-old in America knows Canned Fruit."

"All right, then it'll have to be Canned Fruit. Now here's what I want you to do," she said, as she explained her idea.

"I can't ask them to come over to your place today," Myron protested. "They're busy people . . . stars . . ."

"Just a courtesy call, Myron, from one star to another. Do I have to remind you that I know Johnny Carson personally? And that if you don't help me, I'll have to call him? So please, Myron, you'll call these Canned Fruits. Are they close by?"

"They're at the Drake Hotel. And they have to be at the studio at five-thirty."

"So you'll call them like a good boy, right?"

"Sadie, you're very persuasive. I'll try, but I can't guarantee a thing. I'll call you back."

While she waited for Myron's call, Sadie walked to the window and looked out at the park. She hadn't liked throwing her weight around, but it was necessary. And after all, if Johnny Carson had asked a personal favor of her she'd do it in a minute. She'd run right over and make him a batch of poppy-seed cookies if he wanted them. Or straighten up his apartment, maybe, or whatever. A person who knows another person will help that person if they ask. That's what being a friend is all about, isn't it?

Ten minutes later, Myron was calling. "You're amazing.

They said yes. Ronnie Porter will be there just before three, and he's bringing the other guys, too."

"Oh, Myron, you're a doll. Thanks."

"Don't thank me," Myron said. "They all want to meet you, Sadie. And Ronnie Porter is bringing a copy of your book to autograph. His mother is your biggest fan."

~~~~~~~~~~~~~~~~~

21

When the doorbell rang just before noon, Sadie thought it might be Laura, returning home early from school. To her great surprise and delight, it was Harold Rosenbloom—a tired-looking Harold Rosenbloom. She fell on him with uncharacteristic affection and all but pulled him into the apartment. Rosenbloom's face looked gray.

"Come," she said, "sit down. Can I make you some lunch, Harold? Would you like a cup of tea?"

"A cold drink, perhaps," he said, mopping his face with a snowy handkerchief. Despite the warmth of the day, Rosenbloom was dressed in a white shirt and tie, and was wearing a smart tweed suit, complete with vest. While Sadie went off in search of refreshment, he walked painfully to the living room, leaning heavily on his cane. As if at the end of his energy, he plopped himself down on the couch.

"To what do I owe this treat?" Sadie asked when she had handed Rosenbloom a glass of icy lemonade and seated herself in the facing armchair.

"Business, Sadie. And pleasure, on my part, to see you again. I must say, Mount Eden is not the same place with you gone."

"I'm beginning to miss Mount Eden, too," said Sadie. "But with all these interviews and TV shows, I'm keeping myself busy."

Rosenbloom took a deep sip of his lemonade and then set the glass aside. He opened his worn briefcase and withdrew a sheaf of letters, a legal pad, and a clipboard. "Now then, to business," he began. "Your mail is fascinating, Sadie. Every day, when I open it, I'm never sure what I'll find."

"There are a lot of crazy people in the world, that's for sure."

"And a few smart ones, too." Rosenbloom put on a pair of horn-rimmed glasses and looked at one of the letters before him. "You've been getting the most amazing offers for tie-ins with your book. For instance . . . the Minnesota Vikings would like you to design new warm-up suits for them."

"I see," said Sadie. "And what are the Minnesota Vikings?"

"A professional football team. A good one, too. The only specification they make is that the suit be knitted in the team colors, purple and black. After you design it, they'll arrange for a manufacturer to produce them for the team. They also plan to sell facsimiles to their fans. They're offering quite a bit of money for the design, plus a royalty."

"But what do I know about football?"

"Wait, that's just the beginning." Rosenbloom leafed through some more papers and held one up. "Now here's a conglomerate that's making what I think is an interesting offer. They want to open a chain of knitting shops across the country on a franchise basis. They want to use your name, Sadie . . . and the fee they're offering is substantial."

"My name they want?" She shook her head in disbelief.

"Sadie Shapiro's Knitting Shops . . . It has a certain ring to it, don't you think?"

"Crazy . . ."

"How about this offer? It's from some money men in Dallas, in the franchise food business. Would you believe Sadie Shapiro's Drive-in Restaurants? Featuring something called a knitburger?"

"A *knitburger?* Harold, you're joking."

"They have this idea to make long shoestring potatoes and wrap them around a hamburger so they look like wool."

"Don't tell me any more, I'm getting sick. I wouldn't give my worst enemy a knitburger, and certainly not under my name."

"I have about a half-dozen other offers here, most of them better than the knitburger. People want you to design clothing, to endorse products. You're a hot property, Sadie, and lots of people want to use your name. The point is, someone has to deal with these opportunities, follow them up, nail them down."

"Wait a minute, Harold, I'm still back on the knitburgers," Sadie said, grinning.

"You see now why I came up here, today. There's a lot to be done, and quickly, before some of these offers disappear."

"No, I don't see that," Sadie said. "I don't ask anybody to make me an offer, and as far as I'm concerned we'll still be the same friends if I don't even answer their letters except to say hello."

Rosenbloom stared at Sadie, as if not believing what he had just heard. "Nonsense," he said. "No one turns his back on an opportunity like this. I'm telling you, Sadie, with proper management there's no telling how much could be done. And it wouldn't be terribly difficult, either. There's a bundle of money out there, just waiting to be scooped up."

"Money for what? Who needs money, at my age? With Social Security and Reuben's pension, I've got enough to get by, believe me. Now, all of a sudden, to try to become a millionaire . . ."

"Not you, Sadie, me. I'd make the try and I'd do the work. All you'd have to do is say yes or no once in a while, and sign some papers."

"All to make money. It's crazy, Harold."

"It's not crazy, Sadie. It's the way the world is made."

"Your world, maybe, not mine. I never cared that much about money."

A quiet smile lit Rosenbloom's sallow face. "I've always found that people who say that are usually not in a position to make any."

"Then that makes me an exception," said Sadie.

"Money is money," said Rosenbloom. "It doesn't tell anything about a person, but at least it's a way of keeping score."

"What score? You mean the more money a person has, the better he is? How can I believe that? You know what that makes my Reuben, let him rest in peace, who never managed to make a lot of money. What am I supposed to think, he was a nothing because he wasn't rich? Why, I wouldn't give you a dime for a Rockefeller next to my Reuben . . ."

"Let's not make this personal, Sadie," said Rosenbloom, who had begun to perspire.

"But it is. Listen, if I wanted to be rich, I could have married Al Rosman, don't think I didn't have the chance. The man was in the dairy business, and he was crazy about me. The Prince of Pot Cheese, they called him, with money running out of his ears. But was he kind, like my Reuben? Did he love me the way Reuben did? Everyone thought I was a fool to turn him down, believe me. But there's more to life than money, Harold."

Nodding, Rosenbloom reached for his drink and wet his lips. When he spoke again, the urgency was gone from his voice. "We seem to have begun on the wrong foot," he said. "Let me start again. I want you to be my client, Sadie. If you don't want this to be a moneymaking enterprise, I'll set it up another way. I'll make it a nonprofit corporation. A charity, if you like. The Sadie Shapiro Foundation. And all the money we make, you can give it away for all I care."

"Wait a minute," Sadie interrupted. She looked at Rosenbloom in a strange way. "Am I stupid? Is it you, Harold, who needs to make all this money?"

Rosenbloom chuckled softly, shaking his head. "No. I'm

very well provided for. Which is another reason I'd like to do this. I could trust myself not to squeeze every dime out of it, not to overreach." Slowly, pain showing in his face, Rosenbloom crossed one leg over the other and put his head back against the couch. With his eyes closed, he went on. "Now let me tell you the truth, Sadie. I want to do this because I want to do it. I made a big mistake when I walked out of Weymouth and Lazard at sixty-five. I should have fought them and tried to stay on. Failing that, I should have opened an office for myself and kept my hand in.

"I'm like a piece of machinery, Sadie, left out to rust in the rain. I'm a sick man, I know that, but all I've done for years is sit around and listen to my arteries hardening. That's not good enough. I need more.

"With you as my client, I'd be back in it, don't you see? I would work for you for the pure joy of doing it, and doing it well. I'd be making deals again . . . negotiating, handling affairs of weight and substance . . ."

"You really need to do this, don't you?" Sadie said.

"Like I need air to breathe."

"If you don't mind my saying, you look terrible, Harold. I mean, I'm not sure it's such a good idea, *shlepping* around, working hard again . . ."

"Every day that passes, I'll never live again," Rosenbloom said. He looked away and took off his glasses, rubbing slowly at the bridge of his nose with thin fingers. When he turned back to her, tears stood in his eyes. "I have to do this, Sadie," he said. "And you have to let me. Please, don't make me beg."

"I didn't say no, yet," said Sadie softly. She could not bear to see the look in Rosenbloom's eyes. "Tell me again how it works."

Speaking very slowly, Rosenbloom went on to explain the steps involved in setting up a nonprofit charitable foundation that would derive its income from Sadie's outside endorse-

130

ments and activities. There would come into being a corporation, he told her, and a board of directors. Sadie would head that board, with himself, Sam Beck, Marian, and perhaps Bessie Frankel, if Sadie wished, taking the other seats. Later on, more directors could be added. But even as Rosenbloom spoke and Sadie nodded approval, she could not help feeling somehow trapped. When Rosenbloom had finished, she knew that some part of her would always regret the decision.

"That's the long and short of it," he said, smiling. "I'll send some papers along for you to sign in a few days. You won't be sorry, Sadie. I promise you that."

"I hope so, Harold, for your sake as well as mine."

"The Sadie Shapiro Foundation," he said, smiling. "I can't wait to get started."

~~~~~~~~~~~~~

22

"Myron sent us," the voice in the hallway said.

A tumult of color and texture leaped to Sadie's eyes the moment she opened the door and saw the three young men. She stared at their wild, shoulder-length hair, shaggy beards and moustaches, faded Levi's dotted with bright Dayglo patches, vests of curly animal hide.

"Like, wow," the tall one in front said. "The real Sadie Shapiro. I'm, like, Ronnie Porter and these guys are Canned Fruit."

"Come right in, Mr. Porter . . . and Fruits."

The singing group slouched past Sadie into the living room. Canned Fruit put down the alligator guitar cases they were carrying and looked around. "Man," one of them said, "like straight America, U. S. A."

"Yeah," said the other, "no piano."

"Sit down, sit down," said Sadie. "You want maybe a cup of tea, a piece of fruit?"

"Organic fruit?"

"No," said Sadie. "Apples, pears and nectarines."

"No, thanks," said Porter. He flashed a wide, lopsided grin. "Wow. My mother thinks you're aces. She, like, watches you all the time on the box, you know? And she ran right out and got your book."

"That's nice. Tell her I think she's got a very handsome son."

"Oh, wow," said Porter, "you're beautiful. Like, even at your age, doing your thing. Like, knitting, and everything, with wool and all." He raised his vest and showed Sadie a wide, knotted belt. "I'm into macramé myself, you know. I get this organic hemp flown in from the Philippines. It keeps my hands busy when I'm waiting to go on. You know?"

"Hey, man, ask her if we can smoke," one of the others said.

"Of course, Fruits," Sadie said. She watched Canned Fruit take small, thin, crumpled cigarettes from their vests and light up.

"Tell me about this gig, Mama," Porter said. "Myron said we didn't have to play or anything. Like, what's up?"

Sadie seated herself next to Porter and told him about Laura, her diet, and her general state of unhappiness. "So I figured," she summed up, "to me she wouldn't listen, but to you she would. Together, maybe we can stop this overweight business."

Porter's face grew serious. "Heavy," he said.

"Exactly."

"I dig it. It's like the old 'eat your spinach' bit, right? Okay, I'll lay it on her. When does the chick get here?"

"Any minute." A cloud of smoke from Canned Fruit's cigarettes rolled in Sadie's direction. Her nose wrinkled as she smelled the strange odor. "What is that?" she asked.

"What is what?"

"That smell," Sadie said, sniffing again.

Canned Fruit giggled, and Ronnie Porter smiled. "Organic cannabis. We have it flown in from Guatemala. It costs, like, a small fortune."

"That's a funny brand of cigarettes—cannabis," said Sadie as Canned Fruit broke up. "I never heard of it."

"Yeah, well, they don't sell it everywhere," Porter said.

They heard the sound of a key turning in the front door, and Laura came in. The girl walked to the living room and stopped dead in her tracks, her mouth open.

133

"Laura," Sadie said, getting up, "we have some visitors. They came especially to see you and me."

"Oh, wow," said Laura, her eyes wide and bright.

"This is Ronnie Porter, and those are Canned Fruits. I'd like you to meet Laura Wall."

"Oh, wow," said Laura.

Porter grinned at Laura and stood towering over her. She seemed rooted to the floor. "Yeah, well," he said, nodding. He helped her off with her knapsack. "I've heard a lot about you from Sadie, here. So like, hello."

"You *know* Sadie?" asked Laura, her voice rising a few octaves.

"We're, like, old friends. In show biz, and all, you know." He turned and winked at Sadie.

"Oh, wow," said Laura. Like a zombie, she let Porter lead her into the room and sat down beside him. "Oh, wow," she said.

"Oh, man," said Porter, "look at them eyes. She's like a madonna, Sadie, you know? How about this chick, guys?"

"Yeah," said one Fruit. "Oh, wow," said the other. Then they giggled.

"Like if we needed a chick out front in the act, you would be it, Laura."

"Oh, wow," said Laura.

"Stand up," said Porter, "and turn around slow. Let me look on you good, you know?"

Still looking dazed, Laura stood and modeled for Porter. He looked at her appraisingly, nodding. "You remind me of somebody," he said.

"Who?" said Laura.

"Mama Cass," he said, and Laura's face fell in. She blinked her eyes and bit her lip.

"Yeah," said Porter, "that's the way you come on. Like Cass Elliot. A little doll face on top of a big body. Beautiful."

Laura stood gazing at Porter, her face working. Then a tear, just one, rolled slowly down her left cheek.

"Hey, Laura, what's the matter? Did I say something wrong? I mean, I figured you want to look the way you look, you dig? Don't you?"

"No-oo-oo," she said, covering her face with her hands. Then she really started crying in earnest. Sadie rushed in and drew Laura to the couch, cradling the little girl in her arms. She stroked her hair and made soothing noises, clucking into her ear.

"Oh, wow," said Porter, "like, forgive me. I didn't know. I mean, I figured maybe fat was your thing."

As these last words hit home, Laura began to wail. "Sha," said Sadie to her. "Sha, sha."

"I-don't-want-to-be this way," Laura sniffled. "I don't! I don't!"

"This is an ugly scene, man," one of the Fruits said. "The worst," said the other.

"Hey, Laura, listen," Porter said. "Like if you don't want to be fat, hey, then don't be. I mean, fat can be beautiful if you like it, see? But if you don't, then maybe it can be ugly."

"Body pollution," said the first Fruit.

"Yeah. Like, stick with the real things and lay off the chemicals. You know, pick up on yoghurt and wheat germ and nuts. Things like that, Laura, and it won't take long to get straight. You'll see."

"Hey, man, let's split," said the second Fruit.

As Laura took her face from Sadie's shoulder, Porter flashed her a grin and a V-sign. "Goodbye, Laura," he said. "Sadie, you keep in touch and let me know how she's doing." Gathering the Fruit, he led them to the door.

Their departure was Laura's signal for still more tears.

135

"Oh, Sadie," she cried, "I don't want to look like I do. I don't want to be fat. But what am I going to do?"

Sadie smiled to herself as she stroked the girl's hair, then held her close in a tight and affectionate hug. "What are you going to do? Laura, I thought you'd never ask."

23

~~~~~~~~~~~~~~~

He wandered like a sleepwalker from the shade trees in the back garden to the top-floor solarium and downstairs again. Now he was sitting in the social hall, holding a fistful of cards as Abe Farkas stared at him. "Beck, throw a card."

Sam Beck sighed heavily, the ever-present cigar for once dead in his left hand. "I am a man bereft," he said.

"You are a man asleep," said Farkas. "Throw a card."

"Go figure a woman of indeterminate age, a widow no less, is going to be concerned about her chastity. Farkas, how can you explain something like that?"

"You explain it, Beck. Meanwhile throw a card already."

"Believe-It-Or-Not-Ripley wouldn't believe a thing like this. I mean, what am I, a dirty old man?"

"You want to have a discussion group, Beck, or you want to play cards?"

"Six months ago I had a friend, a companion. Now I got a TV star turned into a bluenose. That book, Farkas, that started all my troubles. Before she wrote that book she was just Sadie Shapiro. Now, she's *the* Sadie Shapiro!"

"Beck, you going to keep that card or not? Tell me soon or I swear I'm going to fall asleep."

"Living in an apartment with her editor and a little girl. I mean, is that better than moving in with me? Ridiculous. And the more I don't see her, the more I'm burning up inside to be with her. We could be so happy, Farkas. How much longer can I wait?"

137

"Beck, what day is today? We've been playing so long I forgot."

"Farkas, I'm telling you, I'm getting crazy."

"That makes two of us. Beck, *will you throw a card!*"

"Who can think about cards? I'm going out of my mind. Mark my words, Farkas—I may do something desperate. Something wild. Because Sadie Shapiro has turned me into a crazy person."

"I give up," said Farkas.

Beck looked down at the cards in his hand, his mind far away. Almost without thinking, he selected a card and threw it face down on the table, then laid down the rest of his hand. "Gin," he said.

One of the major changes wrought by the runaway success of *Sadie Shapiro's Knitting Book* could be seen in the carpet at the foot of Arnold Hawthorne's desk. The old rug, bare spot and all, had been torn out by the roots and replaced. The publisher's desk was gone, too, and he now sat behind a $3,000 imported teak design that all but dwarfed the room. "All right now," he said as Marian and Jack Gatewood seated themselves on the old, stained couch, "let's get the weekly Sadie Report up to date. Jack, why don't you fill me in on the sales picture?"

"Right. Sales are still holding strong at about 7,000 copies a week. Sold to date, sixty thousand. Back orders in the house of fifty thousand. Really, Arnold, the only problem we have is producing books fast enough."

"Splendid. What about the book club, foreign rights and reprint sale, Marian?"

"Well, the Book-of-the-Month *and* the Literary Guild both took it, as you know. In addition, the Arts and Crafts Book Club will make it a major selection next month.

"It's been sold in England and France, so far, and we have three German publishers bidding for it even as we speak. I've had nibbles from four paperback publishers. My guess is they will probably all bid on it, and that the rights should bring us between one hundred fifty and two hundred thousand dollars. That's a conservative estimate, by the way."

"Wipe your mouth, Arnold," said Jack. "You seem to be drooling."

"Arnold," Marian began, "have you actually totted all this up? I mean, do you have an estimate of what Sadie has earned thus far?"

"Oh, I'd say offhand that she's earned back her advance," Hawthorne said with a wide smile. "Plus a little more. Say about a hundred thousand dollars."

"Say about a hundred *twenty-five* thousand dollars," Jack said instantly. He shook his head and slowly smiled. "Dirty pool, Arnold."

"Every penny will be accounted for," the publisher said heavily. "I was only speaking roughly, you understand. Now then, tell me about Sadie's promotional tour. When do you and Sadie leave?"

"In two months. The first stop is Cleveland, and then we'll work our way West."

"And how long will you be away?"

"As long as sales hold up. At least three or four months, possibly longer. We'll be coming back to tape some TV shows in New York from time to time. And pick up some clean underwear."

"Very good," Hawthorne said. "We'll miss you, Marian. But your cause is just, not to say profitable."

"Speaking of just causes," Marian smiled, "there's something I'd like to take up with you. A promotion and a raise, not necessarily in that order."

"Jack, I think you'd better leave us," Hawthorne said.

"Why should he leave? He's the editor-in-chief."

"And he's a soft touch, too, Marian. If it were up to him

you'd be sitting behind this desk and I'd be out on the road peddling books."

"Bye, Marian," said Jack. "Give him hell." The door closed softly behind him.

"Now then, Marian, what's on your mind?"

"Money, first of all. I make thirteen thousand a year. It's not enough. I want twenty-five."

"Twenty-five!" the publisher exploded. "Are you crazy?"

"Just waking up, Arnold, not crazy. And I want to be made a vice president, as soon as you can manage it. So that Mace Masterman and Eustace Fielding and the other editors around here know there's a brand new pecking order."

Arnold Hawthorne's face had gone sallow, and he slumped in his swivel chair. "How low of you, Marian," he said. "To blackjack me just when we're starting to get Harbor Press back on its feet."

Marian laughed, enjoying herself at the publisher's discomfiture. "Arnold, you are simply incredible. I can't talk money with you when business is bad, and now you tell me I'm taking advantage when business is good. It's really funny, Arnold."

"Marian, my dear, loyal Marian. Stabbing me in the back."

"Between the eyes, Arnold. And I'm not your dear, loyal Marian. That's the old dishrag routine you practiced on me for years. I've grown up now. I don't handle the switchboard anymore or go downstairs for coffee, remember? And what I've been doing is carrying this place on my back for years without being paid for it."

"We all love you, Marian. I think you're aware of that. And we've always appreciated what you—"

"Then put it in an envelope, Arnold. Pay me and promote me. I think that's a marvelous way to express your love and affection."

The publisher shook his head so hard his jowls swung.

"Twenty-five thousand dollars. It's absurd. I don't know what's got into you."

Marian threw back her head and laughed. "I think I know what's got into me, strangely enough. A little of Sadie Shapiro, Arnold. Some of her spirit and her energy. A touch of her confidence. Work side by side with Sadie and some of it begins to rub off on you."

"You are holding me up, Marian, and you know it."

"Careful, Arnold. You are talking to Sadie Shapiro's editor. I can't tell you how fantastic it feels to walk into a restaurant and have people begin to buzz about you behind their menus. A lot of people have been calling me lately. Editors, publishers . . . for the first time in my life, Marian Wall is in demand."

"Marian . . ."

"Twenty-five thousand, Arnold, not a penny less."

The publisher swallowed hard. As he slowly nodded, his face looked gray.

"And the vice presidency."

Hawthorne's cheeks ballooned and a puff of air came out of his mouth.

Marian looked at her watch. "Yes or no, Arnold. I have an important appointment."

Hawthorne was a beaten man. "You win," he said, raising both hands in a sign of surrender. Marian swooped down on him and kissed his cheek. "You won't regret it, Arnold," she said, kissing him yet again. "And now I've really got to run."

Hawthorne looked at her with a critical eye. "Where are you going? Who's trying to hire you away?"

Marian's face seemed to glow. "I'm going to Mr. Freddie. In ten minutes I'm going to get myself one hell of a haircut."

Hawthorne was actually groaning when she dashed out of his office.

141

~~~~~~~~~~~~~~

24

The two figures rounded the corner of the track alongside the reservoir in Central Park and slowly headed for home. From a distance, they almost appeared to be twins. Upon closer inspection, however, the differences between them became apparent. The older one was thinner, more energetic, and jogged along in perfect form. The young girl in the matching sweat suit seemed to bounce rather than jog, and her straining face had turned bright red.

"Just a little more, Laura dear, we're almost home," Sadie said. "That's it, on the flat of your foot, not your heels."

"Sadie," puffed Laura, "I think I'm dying."

"A little more, nice and easy. Am I jogging too fast?"

"No. I am." Laura groaned and wiped the rivulets of sweat from her face with the back of her hand. "When I take a step, everything bounces."

"There's more to bounce with you, Laura," Sadie said. "But that's good. Every bounce is breaking up the fat. Think of it that way."

"I can't think," said Laura, slowing down. "My brains are scrambled."

"All right, let's walk a little. Until your breath comes back."

"Sadie, don't get mad, but this jogging is making me hungry. What's for dinner?"

"Food is your enemy, remember that, Laura."

The girl swallowed hard, then nodded. "No dinner, okay."

Sadie laughed and threw an arm around Laura. "I didn't

mean *no* dinner. Of course you'll have dinner. Dieting doesn't mean fasting. It only means starving a little. Let's see . . . tonight you'll start off with a big dish of carrot and celery sticks, health style."

"What's that?"

"With salt. Followed by a hamburger."

"Oh, wow! With french fries?"

"Without even a bun, cookie. A plain broiled hamburger on a plate, with lettuce and tomato salad."

"Yuch!"

"And for dessert, all the cottage cheese you can eat."

Laura's nose twitched, and a look of pure pain crossed her face.

"Never mind making faces. What do you think, skinny comes easy?" Smiling, Sadie bounced up and down on her toes, put herself in first gear and started into motion. "Jogging time, let's go. Last one across Central Park West is a rotten egg!"

"Oh, madame!" cried Mr. Freddie with a sweeping gesture of the hand, "we have captured you, is it not so?" Mr. Freddie's mouth widened, and with a dazzle of teeth, he smiled at Marian in the mirror.

Vibrating in every fiber of her being, Marian sat straight upright in the upholstered chair and looked at the unfamiliar face staring back at her from the mirror. Oh, my God, a shrill voice in her brain cried, what has he done to you? Where did all that hair go—the mass of brownish matter that you once curled and uncurled, that hung like limp spaghetti around your ears and down onto your shoulders? For there was perhaps an inch of hair left on her head, brushed flat and swept away to the side so that for the first time in ages her forehead was exposed to the stark light of day.

"Magnifique!" cried Mr. Freddie, whooping it up in be-

143

half of the client who seemed to have lost her voice. "It is a new you."

"Y-yes," Marian said at last, a sickly smile on her face. Mr. Freddie swept the covering sheet away and Marian rose, her eyes still riveted upon her own mirror image. Horrible, she thought, terrible. For with the scalping her nose seemed to have grown at least four inches, and the dark rings that targeted her eyes showed much more clearly than ever before. It was not a haircut. It was a disaster.

Marian made a fumbling pretense of appreciation and tipped the fawning Freddie outrageously. Almost whimpering, she made her way to the cashier, wishing she had had the presence of mind to bring a scarf along with her.

With trepidation she stumbled out onto the street, her eyes downcast. Thoughts tumbled through her mind, most of them nauseating. The confidence which had lately blossomed within her had withered and died.

She walked along the building line, peeking at her reflection in the store windows from time to time. Blast Sadie and her ideas, she thought. You have become a fool and a laughing stock. You look ridiculous. Ah, came the compensating thought, but you are a ridiculous vice president at twenty-five thousand per annum, no less. Perhaps if she wore a different dress . . .

On the Fiftieth Street side of Saks she paused and dared a long look in the window, not seeing the clothes but only her own reflection. She had always hated this dress. It had never done anything for her, even when it was new.

On impulse, Marian turned into the store, went to the seventh floor, and quickly bought a $150 pants suit in a quiet oxford-gray.

Contemplating herself in the dressing-room mirror, she decided she had to wear the suit immediately. It helped. Not a lot, but it helped.

"Shall I wrap the dress you came in with?" the salesgirl asked.

"Burn it," said Marian.

Somewhat more confident, she made her way back to the Grindl Building. As she paused at the reception desk to pick up her telephone messages, the girl behind the switchboard stared at her briefly. "What can I do for you, sir?" she asked.

"It's me," Marian said tremulously, "Marian Wall."

The girl stared at her, cheeks flushing pink. "Oh . . . Marian . . . you look different."

Groaning, Marian fled to the corridor and in her haste almost collided with Jack Gatewood. He gaped at her wordlessly. "Marian? Is that you?"

"I'm . . . not sure," she managed to say, wanting to find a hole and drop into it.

"I like your suit. And you've done something . . ." Jack's eyes explored Marian's face and came to rest on her hair. "Oh, no," he said, "you didn't."

"No. Mr. Freddie did."

Jack stepped back in the narrow corridor, his face grave. "But I liked your hair," he said, his voice earnest. "I've always liked your hair. I've always thought that your hair was one of the most beautiful . . ." At this, his hand flew to his mouth and he flushed beet-red. "Sorry . . . I . . . didn't . . ."

Marian worked all afternoon with the door to her office firmly closed. She waited until dark before leaving for home and slunk into the apartment like a whipped cur. Sadie and Laura were sitting in the kitchen when Marian at last found the courage to show herself in the doorway.

"Don't say a word, either of you," she commanded. In an attitude of abject despair, she settled into a chair at the table.

Sadie's mouth opened and closed three times before she could put her voice into operation. "Love your suit," she said.

"Yeah, Mom," Laura piped, "groovy."

"Never mind my suit. What about my head?"

"Ay-yi-yi," said Sadie, sadly surveying the damage Mr. Freddie had wrought. "Whoever gave you that haircut should have his head examined. And it's all my fault. I'm the one who got you steamed up to get a haircut because I thought it would help . . ." Sadie's face was even more grave than Marian's. For once she stopped knitting as she stared at the shorn head that sat almost naked before her. "All right, so I was wrong. So it wasn't your hair." She looked at Marian for at least two minutes. "Your eyebrows," she said at last, "let me tell you something about your eyebrows . . ."

~~~~~~~~~~~~~~~

25

"What are all those papers you're signing?" Marian was asking on an evening several weeks later. "They look very official."

"From Harold Rosenbloom. He makes x's and I sign my name. It's for the foundation, some kind of contracts. He sent them up here today. You should have heard him on the telephone. He was laughing and telling jokes. Can you imagine? Harold Rosenbloom telling jokes?"

"No, I can't."

"He's in his glory, Marian. He made his old firm give him a room with his name on it, and two days a week he goes to Wall Street. He met with those football people today. The Minnesota somethings, they call them."

"Vikings, they call them. And I love your design for their warm-up jackets. I'm sure they will, too. And while we're on the subject of designs, I think it's time to start thinking about a sequel to the knitting book."

"I already have," said Sadie. "At least, I got a title. 'Sadie Shapiro's *Other* Knitting Book,' we should call it, so people don't get it mixed up with the first one. What do you think, cookie?"

"Perfect," Marian grinned.

As the women smiled at each other, Laura came into the living room, ready to have Marian see her to bed. In the few weeks she had been dieting a marked change had taken place. Her cheeks no longer ballooned and the heavy swell of her waist was fast disappearing. The little girl kissed Sadie and went off to her bedroom with Marian.

Where are you, Sam Beck, thought Sadie, as she sat alone in the living room. You haven't called me in two weeks. I'd like to take a walk with you, or go out to a movie, or just sit and talk for a while. There was something about the man that was endearing. You always had a smile on your face when you were around Sam Beck.

Because she was on the couch, Sadie didn't even have to get up to answer the telephone when it rang. "Just you and me," the voice began, "and the sound of waves breaking on the shore. Alone on a lonely beach, I turn and take you in my—"

This time Sadie didn't hesitate. "Is that so, filthy face?" she purred into the phone.

There was a cough on the other end and a quick intake of breath. "Oh, God, I did it again," Heathcliff said. "Forgive me. I didn't mean to—"

"Oh, I know what you meant," said Sadie, "and you should be ashamed of yourself."

"Yes, I know," said Heathcliff after a brief pause. "Look, would you call Marian to the phone? I have to talk to her."

"I should call Marian to the phone to talk to a maniac? Are you crazy?"

"Of course I'm crazy, we both know that. Now would you call her please?"

Sadie stared at the telephone in her hand for a moment. This is altogether a strange person, she thought, and maybe even worse. She was hesitating, holding the phone at arm's length, when Marian came back into the room. "It's that crazy person from the other day, Marian," Sadie said. "Now he even knows your name."

Marian stared at Sadie, then dropped her eyes, blushing furiously. "I'll take it in my bedroom," she said, breaking into a run and closing the door behind her.

Sadie's mouth dropped open and just as quickly closed. The telephone seemed to be burning in her hand. She heard Marian pick up the extension phone in her bedroom, heard her begin to exchange some words with the insane caller. Unbelieving, she listened for a moment before putting down the phone. There was no doubt in her mind now. Marian not only knew the man on the phone, she had spoken with him before.

Marian's face was flushed when she finally emerged from the bedroom. She lit a cigarette and sat down in the armchair that flanked the couch. Clearing her throat, she looked sidewise into Sadie's staring eyes. "I'm . . . I'm sorry you had to hear that."

"I'm sorry *you* heard it," Sadie said, catching her breath. "*Marian!*" she said at double volume, "are you crazy?"

"Sadie, let me explain . . ."

"Explain!" exploded Sadie. "Talking to a madman, and you're going to explain that?"

"He's not a madman. He's just . . . sort of . . ."

"He's just your ordinary sex fiend, that's what he is. And you, Marian Wall, a mother and an *editor* no less, wanted to talk to him? Marian, I don't understand."

A variety of emotions paraded across Marian's face as she tried to put her lips into motion. "Let me explain," she repeated, before lapsing into silence again.

"Wouldn't budge an inch from here," said Sadie, as if speaking to herself. "This has got to be some terrific explanation."

"Well . . . you see . . . I've been getting calls from him for some time now, Sadie . . ."

"I know. I had the misfortune of hearing him two weeks ago."

"Well, it's been more than two weeks. You see . . ."

"How long has he been bothering you, Marian? A month? Two months?"

"It's been a year, actually."

"Dear God!" cried Sadie.

"Perhaps a little longer than that . . ."

"Over a year! Talking to a crazy?"

"Fourteen months, I think. About that long . . ."

Sadie seemed to levitate from the couch. "Marian Wall, are you out of your mind?"

"Sometimes I wonder," said Marian.

"Never mind," commanded Sadie. "You're calling the police, and that's that. I insist. If you think I'm going to stay in this apartment while you're getting calls from some kind of sexual herbert . . ."

"Pervert," corrected Marian automatically, "and he's not. I'm sure of it, Sadie."

Sadie cast her eyes at the ceiling and began speaking to it. "She's getting phone calls from some maniac for fourteen months, and with her that's all right. I ask you, who's crazy around here?"

"Maybe he's sick, Sadie, but not crazy."

"You'll pardon me if I don't understand the difference."

"People who make calls like that seldom do anything violent. The release is in the phone call itself, don't you see?"

"Marian, if he wants a release let him talk to the warden. Call the police, Marian, I'm telling you. A man like that—he knows your name and where you live—God knows what he'll do some day, and you have a child in the house, not to mention me, who wouldn't exactly enjoy waking up to see some Bluebeard standing over my bed."

"He's only after me, Sadie, I'm sure of that."

Sadie hugged her knees to keep herself from jumping up. "Marian, cookie," she began again, holding her voice down, "why do you want to fool around with a man who makes crazy phone calls? Why, Marian, tell me?"

Marian chuckled without mirth. "That's very hard to explain. You see . . . well, there aren't a lot of men exactly chasing me at the moment. Not for years, if we're speaking the truth. And this one—I call him Heathcliff, by the way—he's the only man in my life. And has been for a very long time . . .

"I don't know, perhaps it's silly, but I've sort of gotten used to speaking with him. There's something—in his voice or his manner—that reminds me of someone. And maybe I like that fact that he's so romantic."

Sadie groaned and put her head back against the couch.

"It sounds mad, Sadie, and it is hard to explain, I know. But I do know he's harmless, you see. And I don't mind humoring him. I even enjoy it, sometimes. So I couldn't call the police. It wouldn't be fair after all this time."

"I can't believe I'm hearing this," said Sadie.

"What is it I remember you saying, Sadie, when I met you? Yes—'we all have our ways and that's it.' Well, Heathcliff has his ways and I have mine. And that's why I can't call the police."

"Got a girl here likes talking to a maniac," said Sadie to the ceiling.

"Not a maniac, Sadie. Far from it. He's . . . warm and creative. You know, the things he's always saying sound as if they came right out of a book. I can't take that seriously."

"How about rape?" asked Sadie. "Can you take that seriously? With maybe a lot of hitting and hurting?"

"That's not the Heathcliff I know. He's not violent, I'm sure."

"Oh, boy, you really *like* talking to him."

"I didn't think you'd understand," said Marian, sighing.

"I don't think Joyce Brothers would understand—how do you like that?" Visibly upset, Sadie rose and began striding swiftly from the room.

"Sadie? Where are you going?"

At the doorway, Sadie turned. "To make myself a cup of

151

tea. Because if I sit there any longer I'm going to be crazy, too."

Several hours, and many cups of tea later, they were still talking.

"I surrender about the police"—Sadie was saying—"Okay? If you don't want to get this crazy person arrested and get all involved with jail and everything, I understand. But why don't you just hang up on him when he calls? In a week or so he'll get the message and never bother you again."

Marian grinned over the edge of her mug of tea. "That's just it. You used the word 'bother,' not me. He doesn't bother me."

"So you won't turn him in to the police and you won't chase him away, right?"

"Right."

"And as far as you're concerned, you'll go on talking with him as long as he's interested, right?"

"Right."

"Hmm," said Sadie, thinking out loud, "then there's only one thing left to do, Marian."

"And what's that?"

It was Sadie's turn to grin now. "Invite him up to meet you, of course."

26

~~~~~~~~~~~~~~~~~~~~

For Marian, the next day passed with glacial slowness. As she worked, her mind kept picturing the scene that might take place that very night. What would he look like? Tall, dark, handsome, sexy-looking? What if he wasn't? What would she do if a short, fair, ugly, pathetic-looking Heathcliff appeared in her doorway with arms open wide? What if he had acne, bad teeth, or a wart on his nose? And what would happen if her assessment of his intentions was wrong? How does one handle a rapist, anyway?

Forget it, she told herself as she tried to concentrate on her manuscript, Heathcliff probably wouldn't show up at all.

For Sadie, the approach of dusk made her more and more uncertain. What had she done? What would happen if a masked intruder rushed in when they opened the door? No matter what Marian thought, such men are dangerous. He could kill them all. Just to be on the safe side, Sadie inveigled Laura into spending the night with one of her school chums who lived in the building. Alone in the apartment she looked through the kitchen's assortment of knives, and other deadly instruments, then rejected them. She didn't think she had the ferocity needed to actually use a knife if the time came. No, she said, you live by the knitting needle, and if you have to die by it, so be it. Nevertheless, she did take the precaution of finding her very longest and strongest needle and having it handy.

At dinner, neither Marian nor Sadie ate with much appetite. The problem of what they might face lay like a greasy

153

doughnut on Sadie's chest, and even her customary hot tea did little to calm her nerves.

"He probably won't call," Marian said, her voice edgy.

"He'll call."

"Yes. I suppose so. He almost always does." Marian lit yet another cigarette. "He probably won't decide to come here, though."

"He'll come."

"But what if he doesn't? I mean, we can't be sure he'll take the invitation."

"He'll take it," Sadie said.

"Yes," Marian nodded, her hand shaking. She took a deep drag on her cigarette and began to cough. "Sadie . . . what should I tell him?"

Sadie's eyebrows rose, and she seemed to smile with her eyes. "What you tell him, Marian," she said slowly, "is what he's been waiting to hear."

Marian nodded briefly, her lips pursed. "Yes. I suppose that's the only way." She swallowed hard. "Listen . . . ah . . . I don't suppose you'd want to talk to him? I mean, just to ask him over?"

"You're the one who's experienced with maniacs, Marian," Sadie said. "I mean, with me he's not a personal friend."

As the telephone began to ring, they both jumped about six inches. Leaping up, they stared at each other, then reluctantly turned toward the living room. It was something like a turtle race on the way to the telephone, with Marian hanging back and Sadie pushing her gently. At last Marian picked up the phone.

"I ask for the taste of your sweet lips on mine," Heathcliff was saying.

Marian's wide-opened eyes blinked, and she nodded at Sadie. "Ho . . . ho . . . hold on . . ." At top speed, Marian disappeared into her bedroom, closing the door behind her.

When Sadie heard Marian pick up the bedroom extension, she put the phone down like a hot knish.

In a panic of excitement, Sadie rushed to the front door and checked to see that all three locks were locked. Then she turned and raced for the window in the study, where the fire escape was located. Her hands were actually locking the window shut when she realized what she was doing. Wait a minute, she said to herself. You're not supposed to keep Heathcliff *out*. You're going to be letting him *in*.

A sudden weakness buckled her knees. My God, they were going to actually let a maniac into the apartment. And it was all her own idea.

She heard Marian calling and headed back to the living room. Her face an off-white shade, Marian stood in the bedroom doorway. "He'll be here in ten minutes."

With a whoosh of escaping air from her lungs, Sadie took a staggering half-step forward and sank into an armchair. Was she wrong, or had her heart really stopped beating?

"Sadie!" Marian gasped. She rushed across the room and knelt before the old woman. "Sadie, please . . . are you all right?"

"Not to worry," Sadie said, one hand massaging her chest. "There it is, I'm fine. It only happens maybe once or twice a year. Mainly when I get scared to death. In another minute I'll be a hundred percent. Meanwhile, tell me about Heathcliff."

"Are you sure you're all right?"

"Ipsy-pipsy. Tell me what he said when you invited him over."

"It was very strange, Sadie," Marian said, her head cocked to one side. "I had the feeling he must have been waiting for that invitation for a long time."

"What did you say? I mean, how did you put it, exactly?"

"I just told him to hurry right over . . . that I was waiting. And he said, 'Oh, I'll be right there.'"

"Just like that? So simple? And how did he sound?"

"Strange. As if he were in a trance. Very calm."

"Oh, boy," said Sadie, "that's a bad sign. When a maniac gets very calm, you're in big trouble."

Marian stared briefly at Sadie. "I was thinking the same thing."

"Marian, maybe this wasn't such a terrific idea."

"Now you tell me," said Marian, standing up. She grasped Sadie's hand and helped her to her feet.

Turning away, Sadie walked to her knitting bag and found the needle she had selected. She showed it to Marian. "I'll be standing behind the door with this. One false move and . . ." She made a long thrust with the knitting needle that drew a smile from Marian. "Whatever you do, Marian," Sadie counseled, "don't let him see how scared you are. Never let a maniac know you're scared. It makes them crazy."

"I'll remember that," Marian said. "It's funny. Half of me wants to get Laura's hatchet, and the other half wants to put on more Arpège."

Sadie nodded and began to pace the floor, the hand holding the needle behind her back. "All right," she was saying, "soon we're going to know." Marian was just sitting down to light a cigarette when the doorbell rang. Springing up, she exchanged a terrified look with Sadie. On tiptoe, Sadie gingerly approached the front door and flattened herself to the wall alongside it.

With trembling hands, Marian held the doorknob. "Who is it?" she asked in a voice that was barely a whisper.

"The telephone man," came a voice from the hallway.

Marian took a last look at Sadie and then unlocked all three locks. She opened the door a crack and peered out. "Oh, no!" she cried, stepping back in anguish and shock. "No!" With a strangled cry, Marian turned and ran to her bedroom.

Sadie stood hidden behind the half-open door, a finger held to her lips in alarm. Summoning all her courage, she drew herself to the doorway and looked out. Standing there motionless, his eyes downcast and hands nervously working the brim of a straw hat, was a man she had met many times before.

At last he looked up and met her eyes. "I'm . . . sorry," said Jack Gatewood.

27

"Mr. Gatewood!" Sadie gasped, "it's you." She stared open-mouthed for perhaps a second or two. "But it can't be you. You're . . . you're an *editor-in-chief!*"

A grim smile played about Jack's mouth as he looked away from Sadie's searching eyes. His tall body slumped in an attitude of defeat.

At least half-a-dozen contradictory thoughts flashed through Sadie's mind as she regarded the man in the hallway. It was shocking, it was unbelievable, it was inexpressibly sad. Jack Gatewood, the handsome and gentlemanly editor-in-chief of Harbor Press, was a man who went around making crazy phone calls on the side. Sighing at the impossibility of such a situation, she stepped aside and opened the door halfway. "As long as you're here," she said, "you might as well come in."

Jack's haunted eyes came up to meet hers for a brief instant. Like a robot, he slowly walked into the front hall. "I'm sorry," he said.

"You're sorry and I'm sorry," said Sadie, "but most of all, Marian's sorry. So come sit down in the living room." She watched as Jack seated himself on the edge of the couch, and then she settled into an armchair beside him. The ensuing silence seemed to go on forever, broken only by the sounds of traffic in the street and Marian's sobbing.

Sadie stared at Jack, trying desperately to make sense where none was apparent. Such a handsome man, she thought. Always dresses neat. Fingernails clipped and clean.

Talks and acts like a perfect gentleman. Except, of course, that he was a kind of gentleman who calls people up on the telephone and talks crazy. How could such a thing be? Where was the sense of it? What little part of Jack's mind made him act that way?

Jack cleared his throat loudly and brought his eyes up to meet hers. An embarrassed grin split his face. "I'm sorry about all this," he said in a quiet, controlled voice. "More so than you can possibly know. Especially, Sadie, I'm sorry that you were exposed to it. Forgive me, please."

"Forgiven," said Sadie, "don't bother your mind with it."

"Thank you," Jack said. He glanced at his watch. "If you'll excuse me, then, I suppose I'd better be leaving. Will you tell Marian that if she never speaks to me again I'll understand?"

"Wait a minute," Sadie said quickly.

"I'll resign from the firm, of course. It seems the only course, don't you think?"

"Who resign? What resign? I don't understand."

"But don't you see? Marian and I can never work together again. Not now . . . not when she knows . . ."

"Not so fast," countered Sadie. "You're getting way ahead of yourself. I mean, if anyone is the injured party in all this, it's Marian. And she hasn't said two words to you yet. So I think it's a little previous to start talking about resigning, and not talking to each other. First of all, let's get this whole thing straight. You *are* the person who's been calling Marian up on the phone for fourteen months, aren't you?"

Jack's eyes dropped to the rug, and he ran a nervous finger inside his spotless white collar. His "yes" was barely audible.

"Good," said Sadie. "I just wanted to make sure. Because, looking at you, I still can't believe you'd do such a thing. I mean, if you'll pardon my saying it, you really don't look like that type maniac."

Jack's low laugh was bitter. "Guilty," he said, "guilty. And I'm so ashamed I wish I were dead."

"Now, now," Sadie shushed, "let's keep deadness out of this. We're all people in this world, and we all have our own ways. Of course, some are crazier than others . . ." She smiled at Jack, but he was looking away.

"I'll leave now," he said. "Tell Marian she needn't worry about me. I'm going to disappear from her life. I'll go somewhere . . . just drop out of sight. Australia, perhaps. New Zealand . . ."

"Oh, boy," said Sadie, "that's some solution, to run away. Mr. Gatewood," she said, and waited until Jack's eyes came up to meet hers. "Mr. Gatewood . . . whatever you're going to do, wherever you're going to run away, remember: you're still going to be Mr. Jack Gatewood. So stay here, at least until I talk to Marian, please . . ."

Jack's hand went to his breast pocket and extracted a clean white handkerchief. Gently, he brought it up to dab at his brow. Moving slowly, Sadie retreated to Marian's bedroom door. "Don't go away," she said.

Marian lay face down on her bed, crying softly into her pillow. "Marian . . . cookie," Sadie soothed, "listen to me."

Marian's tear-stained face rose. "Jack," she sobbed between cries, "why did it have to be Jack?" Crying bitterly, she threw herself into the pillow once more.

"Look," Sadie said, "it's not the worst thing. At least the crazy person is someone you know. I mean, it's not a total stranger we're talking about."

Marian groaned and turned her face to Sadie. "Tell him to go away. Tell him I never want to see him again. Tell him I resign." With this, she broke into a series of heavy, racking sobs.

Sadie knelt on the edge of the bed and took Marian's sobbing body into her arms, all the while uttering small, cooing sounds. "Dry your tears. And wash your face. And come out and talk to him."

This must have been the wrong thing to say because Marian immediately began to wail. "No! No! Never, Sadie! Ne—ver!"

Sadie sighed and stroked Marian's hair. "The poor man," she said, "he's sitting there like a lost soul, just waiting for you to say a kind word to him. Come, Marian, give a little sympathy."

"Never," Marian sobbed, "make him go away." The volume of her crying increased, making Sadie back off from the bed. She stood near the door, more bewildered than ever, if that was possible. She turned to rejoin Jack, and paused before opening the door. Think, she commanded herself. Shapiro, do your stuff. For beyond Marian's grief-torn wails and Jack's shamefaced guilt, an idea was taking shape. A man like Jack doesn't call a girl like Marian for fourteen months without feeling something for her. And likewise, Marian would not have gone into conniptions on seeing Jack if she didn't hold him in some special place in her heart. Somewhere, somehow, something was definitely doing between the two of them.

Sadie's face was the picture of cheer as she rejoined Jack. "Marian's having a good cry," she reported. "Won't take two minutes, she'll be here to say hello."

At this news, Jack sat up and reached hastily for his hat. "I'd better go . . . I . . . I can't face her, Sadie."

"Pish tosh," Sadie said, "don't make a move. She'll come out, I'll make tea, and we'll all be the best of friends. You'll see, everything will come out right in the end."

"Oh, Sadie," said Jack, sighing deeply, "if it were only that simple. But it isn't. You see . . . I can't . . ."

"Can't what?" Sadie asked. "Look, I got to ask you a question. What do you feel about Marian? I mean, maybe it's not my business, but I have to know."

161

Jack put his hat aside and looked at Sadie. When he spoke, he looked even more handsome than before. "I love her, Sadie. I adore her. I have from the moment I saw her, nine years ago."

Sadie's grin was triumphant. "I knew it in my bones. Of course you love her. Any fool could tell that. I mean, why else would you call up and talk nutty if you didn't feel for her?"

"Yes," Jack said.

"So there's no problem. You love her, and if I'm not mistaken, I think she cares a little for you. So what's a few insane phone calls between friends? I mean, between people who like each other, these things can be forgiven."

"It's not that easy, Sadie. You see, I simply can't . . . I mean, I can't express . . . That is to say, I have great difficulty in . . . in . . ."

"Wait a minute," Sadie said, "take a rest. I want to talk to Marian." Quickly she rose and slipped into Marian's bedroom. Marian was still lying face down on the bed as Sadie had left her, but her sobs were quieter now, and more infrequent. Sadie drew near and waited for Marian to look at her. "Hey, cookie, guess what?" she said brightly. "Jack just told me something that'll make you feel terrific. Marian, he's in love with you."

As if a magic button had been pressed, Marian's quiet sobs turned to wailing once more.

"Wait right here," Sadie said, and fled to the living room.

"All right," she said, sitting down and rubbing her hands together briskly, "I think we're making progress. Now you were telling me about something you can't do, right? What is it?"

With a look of great pain, Jack began to speak. "What I can't do is tell Marian I love her. I simply . . ."

"Wait a minute," Sadie interrupted. "For fourteen months

162

you said all kinds of things on the telephone. And just now, didn't you tell me you loved Marian?"

"That's just it. To you, I can say such things. Or to Marian, over the telephone, disguising my voice and pretending I was someone else. But I can't say it to Marian. Not directly. Not looking at her, or seeing her eyes on me. It's no use, Sadie."

"I don't understand."

"Neither do I," said Jack, "but there it is. When I look at Marian, something just turns off my brain and I'm speechless. There are so many things I want to say, and I can't say any of them."

"I'm getting the picture," said Sadie. "It's got to be something with moofki-poofki, right? I mean, you're a little mixed-up with sex, if you'll pardon the expression."

"No, no," Jack said swiftly. "I'm all right in that depart—"

"Of course," Sadie went on, "moofki-poofki. It can drive even a normal person crazy.

"I remember a great-aunt of mine telling my mother, when she thought I wasn't listening, about her honeymoon and what happened. And how the next morning, when they both came downstairs to breakfast, she just told her husband she wouldn't do that dirty thing again no matter what he said. And her husband, Arthur, because he was a gentleman, never asked her to do it again, either. Thirty-seven years they were happily married, and that's a fact."

"I'm all right with other women, Sadie," Jack said, blushing. "Take my word for it, there's never been a problem. Until Marian came along. I knew she was different as soon as I saw her, and the more deeply I came to love her, the harder it was to tell her . . . or hint at it . . . or touch her lovely hair." A warm smile crossed Jack's face. "I've always loved her hair, Sadie. Haven't you?"

"Her best feature," Sadie nodded, barely able to hold herself in check. Her hair! Jack loved Marian's hair. If that wasn't a true expression of deep and abiding love, what was?

"The crisis began little more than a year ago," Jack was saying. "I knew Marian was unhappy over her work in the office, and I feared she might leave Harbor Press. I knew I had to act, to say something about how I felt, but I couldn't. One night, after I had been walking the streets for hours, I went home and picked up the telephone to call her. But when I heard her voice, I panicked. I hung up without speaking."

"Ahah! But that gave you an idea."

"Yes. A few nights later I felt myself being drawn to the telephone. As I dialed Marian's number, strange thoughts went through my head. And when I heard her voice, it was as if another person possessed me. The voice I spoke with was not my own. The words I was saying . . . I don't know where they came from."

"Amazing," said Sadie, "like a Dr. Jekyll was hiding in you."

"If Marian had refused to speak to me then, I don't know what might have happened. But she didn't. She listened, and even spoke back to me."

"Is that a wonderful girl?" Sadie said. "She's an angel."

"And so I kept calling. Once a week, in those days. More frequently as time went by. I even had another telephone installed in my office so I could call her during the day. But the past few months, this feeling inside me has become overwhelming. I call her every day now. Sometimes two or three times a day."

"Love comes out in funny ways," Sadie observed. "I had a friend once, her husband used to punch her on the arm every day before he went to work. If a few days went by and he didn't give her a good smack, she used to worry."

"And so when Marian spoke to me tonight and asked me to come here, I was ready. I didn't want to come here, but I had to, if you understand that. Somehow Marian had to know that that person on the telephone was me—another part of me, perhaps, but me all the same. And the devil take me if it turned out badly."

"It was very brave of you," Sadie said, "and here you are. And behind that bedroom door is Marian. Now all you have to do is get up and go in there and tell her what you already told me."

Jack reached for his hat and fingered it briefly. His voice, which had risen in volume as he told his story, was now low-pitched. "Ah, but that's just it, Sadie. I can't do that. I can't speak to her."

"What's so hard to do? You walk in there, sit down on the bed, and tell her all about it."

"Oh, Sadie," Jack sighed, "I wish I could."

"Well, think about it," Sadie said, "and don't go away." Marian was quietly sitting on her bed, smoking a cigarette, when Sadie came in. Sadie quickly summarized her conversation with Jack, but Marian's expression remained downcast. "I wish I could believe him," she said.

"Believe him, Marian. He loves you, honest and true. A little mixed-up, maybe, but in his heart is only you. For nine years he's been thinking about you."

"And in nine years he's never even hinted it. Except on the telephone, under another name, in another way. How can I accept that?"

"Strange are the ways of love," Sadie said, looking for the moment like an Oriental sage. "Who knows what's laying there in the hearts of men?"

"I just can't accept a secondhand love, Sadie. Not from Jack. If he's loved me for nine years, why hasn't he spoken before now?"

"Marian, please, don't expect miracles. I know, every girl thinks about a Sir Gallahead comes riding along on a white horse and throws maybe a rose at her feet. But where does that happen, except in books? My Reuben, let him rest in peace, never looked like Clark Gable. But an honest, good man he was, with a lot of wonderful ways. I mean, in books they never tell you when it's cold out, a man gets up and puts an extra quilt on you, you shouldn't be cold. A Romeo, what you call it, never gets involved in that. He's always too busy sweeping girls off their feet. But in real life, Marian, what counts is the man who lets you sleep a little later while he gives the kids breakfast."

"No," Marian said with a tilt of her nose, "not Jack."

"Why not Jack? What's wrong with Jack? That's a very nice fella, sitting out there in the living room, phone calls aside. Handsome, right? Quiet and peaceful, with a good head on his shoulders. And for nine years, Marian, that man has loved nobody but you. What more can you want?"

"Passion, Sadie, for one thing."

"Passion is for little girls, Marian, and only once in a while. Believe me, what you should be thinking about is tenderness, being gentle, kindness and consideration, and on the phone he's very passionate."

Marian's look was scornful. "And what do we do when it's time to make love, Sadie? Does he call me long distance, or what?"

"All right," Sadie conceded, "you got a point there. I'll be right back."

"Making a lot of progress," she reported to Jack. "Everything is ipsy-pipsy, except for one little thing."

"And what is that?"

"A little trifle, a piffle, a nothing. She wants you to go in there and tell her how much you love her."

These words could not have had more effect had Sadie slapped Jack in the face. "I thought as much," he said, inspecting the rug. "I've lost, then. The ballgame is over."

"Never," Sadie said, rolling up her sleeves. "A Shapiro never gives up, and neither should a Gatewood. All right

166

now, make believe I'm Marian. Go on. Tell me how much you love me."

Jack's expression was blank as he stared at Sadie.

"Waiting to hear from you," Sadie said. "Come on, a few nice words."

"I . . . can't."

"Think romantic. Say anything."

"Sadie, I . . ."

"I'll turn my back," Sadie said, whirling about. "There, I'm not even looking at you. Make believe I'm Marian."

"I can't do it."

"Off the couch," Sadie commanded. Half-pulling him to his feet, she marched him swiftly across the room. "Pick up that telephone," she ordered.

Jack's face had a sickly look, but he took the instrument in his hand and slowly brought it to his lips.

"Progress," Sadie said. "Now let's hear it."

His mouth opened and closed, but Jack Gatewood had no words.

At top speed Sadie circled the room and extinguished every lamp. In almost total darkness she felt her way back to Jack. Clapping a small but strong hand on his shoulder, she exhorted him: "I'm Marian and you're Heathcliff. Start talking."

There was a moment of silence and then a guttural laugh that made goosebumps rise on Sadie's arm. "I'm holding you at arm's length, looking into your lovely eyes," . . . Jack Gatewood/Heathcliff was saying.

"At last!"

"And I . . . and I . . ."

"Kissing," Sadie prompted as Jack hesitated, "a little kissing is always nice."

"And I . . . reach out and brush your sweet lips with my own. And . . . and . . . and . . ."

"Grab hold and give a hug," Sadie whispered fiercely.

". . . crush you to me, feeling the warmth of your skin, the sweet curve of you molded into my . . .

"Hey," Jack said, in his own voice, "I never got that far before."

Quickly, Sadie pushed him to Marian's closed door. "Keep talking," she said, "whatever you do, don't stop talking."

"I feel possessed by you . . . I sweetly brush the tip of your chin with my lips and kiss your neck . . ."

"He's talking, Marian," Sadie said, half-dragging a reluctant Marian to the door. "He's saying things to you."

"I won't listen."

With a strange cry, Sadie ran to the bed and snapped off the lighted lamp. Finding her way back in the dark, she forced Marian close to the door. "Marian, you've got to listen. Give a man a chance."

"I want to keep kissing you forever, Marian . . . darling, I want to do everything . . ."

"You only get one chance," Sadie was whispering, "and when it comes, you've got to grab it."

"No," Marian's lips were saying, but her ears were tuned to the sweet music that came through the door.

Fifty years of knitting gave strength to the small hand that reached through the half-opened door and grasped Jack Gatewood by the end of his tie.

Twenty years of jogging gave strength to the lean body that pulled him, still talking, through the doorway and into Marian's open arms.

There was the sound of a sharp intake of breath, a quiet sigh of pleasure, and then Sadie was in the darkened living room, her back against the firmly closed bedroom door.

She listened to the silence for a moment, and smiled.

~~~~~~~~~~~~~~~

28

"What do you mean, you don't know where she is?" Laura was saying.

"Finish your breakfast and drink your skim milk," Sadie said. "Look at the time, you'll be late for school."

Laura grumbled into her glass, but polished off the milk in one large gulp. "If Mom's not in the bedroom, why won't you let me look?" she demanded.

"Because Macy's doesn't tell Gimbels, that's why," Sadie countered. "Shoosh now, and off to school. I'll see you at three o'clock."

Over Laura's protests, Sadie saw her to the door and into the hallway. Ten minutes later, dressed in a sweat suit of lavender, Sadie was across the park and circling the reservoir. The air was clear, the morning sun bright over the buildings flanking Fifth Avenue, and as she jogged, feeling strong and free, Sadie's mind went back over the events of the evening before. Not given to self-doubt, she still felt twinges of guilt. Against their will, she had forced two people to do something she, herself, had never done. It was wrong, she knew, but was it? Swept up by the course of events that had brought so many surprises, she had acted out of instinct instead of reason. Jack was made for Marian, she realized now, and maybe vice versa. But the vice in that versa was what troubled and stuck in her mind.

Marian was unmarried, and yet Jack had spent the night with her. According to every belief Sadie held, that was a sin of the worst kind. So why wasn't she more upset? Why was something that was perhaps right for Marian, not right for herself?

What did she really feel for Sam Beck, she asked herself, and what about her firm and fixed ideas of chastity? Thinking hard, she rounded the corner of the reservoir and began jogging back toward home. Central Park was abloom in the bright, early morning sunshine. Young men and women walked their dogs and a few nannies sat beside their baby carriages.

Sam Beck. Living with a man again. Sleeping in the same bed with a man who was not her husband. Would God, looking down, pronounce her a sinner? Would a heavenly thunderbolt be hurled at her the moment she slipped beneath the sheets with Sam? No, probably not, but what would she feel in her heart at that moment? Would that little clock of conscience, ticking away in her for seventy-two or seventy-five years, suddenly come to a stop, its hands frozen in horror, pointing at her in shame?

You are what you are, Sadie, she told herself, and you must do what you must do. But what? How about a specific? Could you give a for-instance?

Sam Beck. She missed him. She wanted terribly to be with him, to look at him, to hear his jokes, to share his sunny disposition. She wanted to feel her hand on his arm when they were out walking, to smell the rich scent of his cigar, to see the shine in his soft, brown eyes when he looked at her in his special way. Love . . . it can make even a smart person crazy, but of the fact that Sam Beck loved her she had no doubt. And what then of Jehovah and the commandments? What was written there of Social Security rules, of insurance policies, of wills, testaments, and the rights of certain beneficiaries? To say nothing of the right to happiness of people who might, in their declining years, rekindle in each other a flame they had long since supposed had died?

On Central Park West, down the block from Marian's

apartment house, she found a bench in the sun and sat down to wait and think. If what Marian and Jack had found last night was real and right—and she thought in her heart it was—then could not Sadie Shapiro and Sam Beck find the same?

All right, suppose they took an apartment. In her mind's eye, she saw it clear. A few bright, sunny rooms, overlooking the park. A cozy kitchen for tea and talk, a few comfortable chairs in the living room, a good light for knitting and reading. And what would the name on the door read, and on the bellpush downstairs, and on the mailbox? Beck/Shapiro? Shapiro/Beck? Two adults, living together without benefit of ceremony? Living as man and wife, except that she would not be a wife.

What would she be, then? Sam Beck's woman? A concubine, at her age? All the ancient words for a woman of such status flashed through her head—words she had heard her mother use with scorn. Yes, that is what she would be, exactly that.

A faint breeze stirred the leaves of the tree above her head and tears filled Sadie's eyes. How could she live with Sam when she could not live with her conscience? How could she not live with him when being apart caused so much heartache?

The door to the apartment house swung wide, and she saw Marian, smiling, step out into the sunshine. Behind her, the door swinging closed as he followed, stepped Jack. Hand in hand, they waited in the sun until Jack managed to hail a taxi. As it pulled away, Sadie saw Marian's head turn to Jack. They were kissing in the back seat as the taxi turned into the park.

Upstairs, Sadie showered and lay down to rest. Mercifully, she slept until noon. Waking, she wandered about the apartment, the heavy weight of her conscience giving her no peace. A dozen times she walked to the telephone to call Sam

Beck, and a dozen times she could not. On her next trip the telephone rang even as she had it in her hand. She heard Sam's voice, but it suddenly sounded hollow, and very far away.

"Prepare yourself, I have bad news," he was saying as Sadie's heart began to sink. ". . . took a nap after lunch . . . I went to wake him . . . passed away in his sleep . . . Sadie, Harold Rosenbloom is dead."

29

Slowly, the crowd of people who had come to mourn filed into the chapel. They shuffled down the long center aisle, their voices hushed by the high-ceilinged room, and seated themselves on the polished wooden benches, leaving the first row empty for members of the immediate family. Holding fast to Sadie's arm, Marian guided her down the aisle and into a pew near the front. Sadie's face was pale and drawn, reflecting the long night she had passed, a night which had brought her neither comfort nor sleep.

Marian had never seen Sadie this way. The old woman's spirit had been crushed by the events of the previous day. She blamed herself for Rosenbloom's death, repeating over and over again: "I did it, it was me . . . I should never have let him go back to work." No matter how hard Marian tried to talk sense to her, she would not be comforted. The guilt she felt was overwhelming, and had overnight etched deep lines in her cheeks.

Two rows behind Sadie sat Sam Beck, Abe Farkas and Bessie Frankel. Many other Mount Edenites were seated throughout the chapel. Down front, Rosenbloom's family filed into the first row. A young, clean-shaven rabbi mounted the altar as the casket was wheeled into place. As he began chanting an ancient prayer, Sadie bent her head, dabbing her eyes with a handkerchief. Marian's arm went around her shoulders, and she pressed Sadie's trembling form to hers.

Twenty minutes later they stood on the sidewalk outside the chapel. Polished black limousines were drawn up in a long line at the curb; the trip to the cemetery was about to begin. Out of the crowd stepped the tall figure of Sam Beck. Wordlessly, he took Sadie's arm and helped her into a limousine, then stood aside as Marian, Bessie and Abe Farkas entered. Throughout the drive he held Sadie's hand and stroked her hair as her friends tried to give her comfort. By the time they stood beside the grave, Sadie was beginning to look and feel better.

The cloudless sky and bright sun mocked the solemnity of the occasion. The prayers and benedictions were recited, a few last words were spoken, and Harold Rosenbloom's body was lowered to its final resting place. Fewer than half the chapel mourners were at the grave site, and as they walked slowly down the grassy slope that led back to the road, Sam Beck drew Sadie aside.

Holding her hand, he led her through a grove of trees to a shaded knoll and sat down with her on a marble bench. "I have a little visit to pay," he said, after a moment. "You'll wait for me here." Sighing, Beck squeezed Sadie's hand and walked a few steps away back up the hill.

In front of a simple headstone, Sadie saw him pause, his head bent. She saw his lips moving, but could not hear his words, and after what seemed a long time, he stooped to pick up a small stone which he placed on top of the monument. He paused then, handkerchief in hand, and wiped at his eyes. Keeping his head averted, he adjusted the lapels of his suit coat and fussed with his tie. When he turned back to rejoin her, he was once more composed.

"All right," he said heavily as he sat down beside her, then lapsed into silence.

"Listen, Sam," Sadie said slowly, "I've been doing a lot of thinking these last twenty-four hours . . ."

"I know," said Sam. "So have I."

"I'll always think about what I did to Harold, how I sent him out to work again, a man so sick . . ."

"Please, Sadie, let it go. You gave him happiness in his last days, and that's what you should remember, nothing more. I was with him every day these last few weeks. I know how pleased he was to have something to do. He was like a different Harold . . . laughing and joking around. Unfortunately, as it turned out, he didn't have that much time left to him. But who could know that, except maybe God?"

Nodding, Sadie reached out and took Sam's hand. Their eyes met, and in another instant she was in his arms, hugging him close to her with all her strength. "Sam," she whispered as she held him, "I got something to say."

"Wait," he said, breaking the embrace and holding her at arm's length. "Let me speak first."

"No, Sam, please. It's been on my mind—"

"Sadie—"

"—about us and the way we want to be together and the way we keep ourselves apart."

"Exactly."

"And over and over in my mind I think it's wrong, I mean I *know* it's wrong, but in my heart a different song is playing . . . and what it's telling me is '*Hey!* Who says you have to be right all the time?' And who says because you hold an idea in your head for seventy-two or seventy-five years, that idea always has to be right?"

"Sweetheart—"

"I mean, I know you got all kinds of good reasons why you can't marry me, which I don't understand at all. I mean, there's children to be thought of, and you already told me about your insurance and your will and everything like that, which I never thought was a good reason, but maybe I'm a little bit in the wrong, too, if you take my meaning, which I see you do because you're smiling in that funny way."

"Are you all finished?" Sam asked.

"No. Only getting started. Sam, I made up my mind. I don't care if it's wrong. I don't care if I'm breaking a law or if people will talk about us or if we'll have a funny name downstairs on the bell, or even if the mailman will know we're living together and we're not a man and wife. Because who knows how long it'll be, or God forbid, how short the time is that's left for you and me to be together. I only know that my heart is filled up with you, with your goodness and your kindness, with that smile that gives me such a feeling inside I want to hug you whenever I see it. I love you, Sam Beck, and I don't care who knows it or what they say, their tongues should get heavy if they say a word to me, but I don't care about anything else in this whole wide world except being with you forever and making you happy, and if that's a sin, then call me sinner, because from this very minute I'm not going to let you out of my sight, and how do you like that?"

As Sadie paused for breath, a strangely fierce look had come over her. Gazing at it, Sam's smile grew even wider. "Are you all finished now?" he asked gently.

To Sadie's surprise, she was.

"All right," Sam said. "Now I'll have my say." Dropping to one knee, he took her hand and pressed it to his cheek. "Sadie," he said, "let's get married."

30

And they did.

Not on The Tonight Show, which was the master publicity stroke Arnold Hawthorne hoped and fought for. And not without an anxious moment or two along the way.

There were so many arrangements to be made, and only two weeks to go before Sadie's promotional tour. There were blood tests ("an old woman like me they're worried about VD, they should be ashamed," Sadie kept saying) and marriage licenses to be arranged. Not to mention the matter of the dresses to be worn by the bridal party. Sadie, of course, wanted nothing more than to sit down and knit them at once. But on this occasion she took Marian's advice, especially when Marian forced Arnold Hawthorne to move forward his royalty payment to Sadie—a little matter of $147,987.03, to be precise.

It was a stunning moment for all concerned, and there shortly followed a new checking account for Sadie, plus a visit to Bergdorf Goodman.

Several days later, on a warm, clear Sunday afternoon, Sadie Shapiro and Samuel Joseph Beck were married in the back garden of the Mount Eden Senior Citizens Hotel in Queens, New York. The bride wore a short cocktail dress of bright blue silk that matched her eyes, and carried a bouquet of pink roses and maidenhair fern. She was attended by her daughter-in-law, Mrs. Stuart Shapiro of Coral Gables, Florida, Mrs. Marian Wall, vice president of the publishing firm of Harbor Press, and by Mrs. Bessie Frankel, a resident of the hotel.

The groom was dressed in a suit of blue serge and wore a string of love beads around his neck, a wedding gift from the flower girl, Miss Laura Wall of New York City.

The ceremony completed under a canopy of white gardenias, the wedding party was sped in a fleet of limousines and one yellow taxi to the Fifth Avenue Presbyterian Church, where the newly joined Mr. and Mrs. Beck stood up for Marian Wall and Jack Gatewood.

A joint wedding reception was held at the Hotel Pierre; media coverage of the dual nuptials was unusually extensive. A host of show business luminaries attended the reception, and the NBC Tonight Show orchestra provided music for dancing. A high point of the evening came with the singing of a traditional Puerto Rican wedding song by Mr. Juan Otero, a personal friend of both couples.

The following day, both wedded couples (and Laura) set off for Kennedy Airport to embark on a combined honeymoon and publicity tour. Jack's plans called for him to spend only the first week with the party, and so his honeymoon was to consist of trips to Cleveland, Dayton, Columbus and Cincinnati, Ohio. Not that it seemed to matter, for both Jack and Marian were so happy they hardly knew where they were most of the time.

As the United Airlines 727 taxied down the runway and prepared to take off, they sat holding hands, with eyes only for each other. Directly behind them, similarly engaged, Sadie and Sam exchanged winks, sharing a wedding night secret only they would ever know.

Gathering speed, the jet aircraft thrust itself noisily into the afternoon sky. Up, up it rose, over Jamaica Bay and began its turn to the west over the streets of Queens.

Far below, as Sadie looked down in awe, the whitewashed brightness of Mount Eden was clearly visible. Laughing, Sadie looked back at Sam and gently squeezed his hand. "An Eden is where you make it," she thought to herself, "and it really could be anywhere."

Then she reached below her seat and took up her knitting.